MISTER SPACEMAN

LESLEY HOWARTH

WALKER BOOKS
AND SUBSIDIARIES
LONDON · BOSTON · SYDNEY

In memory of my mother
Kay Howarth
who made the Spacewalk

With thanks to Mara Bergman

First published 1999 by Walker Books Ltd
87 Vauxhall Walk, London SE11 5HJ

This edition published 2000

2 4 6 8 10 9 7 5 3

This book has been typeset in Sabon.

Printed in Great Britain by
Cox & Wyman Ltd, Reading, Berkshire

British Library Cataloguing in Publication Data
A catalogue record for this book is
available from the British Library.

ISBN 0-7445-7282-7

CONTENTS

... he was a child; but he knew his own soul and treasured it, guarding it as the eyelid guards the eye, and without the key of love he let no one into his heart.

– Seriozha's lesson, from *Anna Karenina*, by Leo Tolstoy

Part One

REACH FOR
THE STARS

Thomas switched on the computer.

FOUND CDROM the screen winked.

The printer woke up with a hum as the familiar menu popped up.

Clicking on SHORTCUT TO GREMLIN NET, then CONNECT, Thomas Moon activated dialup networking without even knowing he'd done it.

DEE-DER-DI-DUM-
-DEE-DER-DER –

The tuneless dialling tone always grated on his nerves. At the same time he felt excited. Once he got connected, *if* he got connected, he knew he could go anywhere. Thomas felt apprehensive. He knew that sound by heart:

– dee-der-di-dum –
needle-beedle-dwer –

He could hear it all over the house if anyone else used the Net. It called to him as he watched TV. It was trying to tell him something – the voice, the *electronic* voice – of messages going out. It was cool the way instructions flashed out over the wires to connect him to any other computer, anywhere, anytime, wherever he wanted to go. Sometimes he asked his dad how email worked, but his dad always said it was digital and remembered a job he had to do. Of course it was just like a phone. But how were the letters sent down the wires to pop up on someone else's screen?

```
THE LINE IS BUSY
PLEASE TRY AGAIN LATER
```

How many times had he seen that box onscreen? Thomas went pink round the ears. Gremlin Net hated him, he knew. Other people posted email before they went to school. But oh, no. Not him. Gremlin Net wouldn't let him.

It was hard not to take it personally.

Hadn't he tried every off-peak time there was? Even when he got connected and wrote his message in "Pandora" ready to send, sometimes Pandora lost it, or it scrolled off MESSAGES OUT or Gremlin Net sent up a handy message in a box saying: DO YOU WISH TO REMAIN CONNECTED? completely obscuring his email when *of course* he wished to remain connected and had been just about to send it; when in *getting* reconnected he'd get in a flap and do something hasty or his message would get overlaid so he couldn't find it.

"Gremlin Net's got a mind if its own," Thomas complained to his dad. "Sometimes it lets me send emails, sometimes it doesn't. Sometimes it bugs out and loses them. Sometimes it cuts me off. Sometimes it tells me I did something wrong. Sometimes it won't *connect*." Thomas tried hard to explain the feelings of frustration and despair that always overcame him when he flipped on the computer and clicked on SHORT CUT TO GREMLIN NET. "Plus," he told his dad, "it's got a stupid name and I hate it."

"It's just a way to send messages."

"I don't care, it hates me," Thomas said. "Why won't it let me send emails?"

"It does let you send emails," his father told him. "You must be doing something wrong."

"What's wrong is, it stops me *deliberately*," Thomas complained.

The way Thomas Moon knew that Gremlin Net hated him was the way it hid messages from him. He knew it hid messages from him because one day he mysteriously found one:

```
Return-Path: <SPM29@starlight.ac.uk
From: "Me"<SMP29@starlight.ac.uk
To: Thomas.Moon@gremlin.net
```

```
Date: Tue 4 Mar 11:27:33 GMTOBST
Subject: Re: your message, Stars in
your eyes
```
MISTER SPACEMAN (said the message)
DO YOU READ?

I READ, Thomas had mailed back urgently.
THIS IS THOMAS MOON — WHO IS MISTER
SPACEMAN?

But an answer never came. Thomas thought
a lot about that message. Were there other
messages he somehow hadn't noticed? This
one had been stale when he got it, tucked away
in an "attached file" he'd had to learn how to
open. The network had sneakily imported it
with a number of messages for his father and
had never even told him. That was Gremlin
Net for you. Underhand. Sneaky. Exciting.

The message had been headed "Re: your
message, Stars in your eyes."

But he couldn't remember sending any
message headed "Stars in your eyes".

An email had been waiting, somehow along
with or *underneath* an email downloaded
already. It hadn't shown up as incoming mail.
It had called him Mister Spaceman. Where had
that message come from?

After he'd stumbled over the mysterious
message hidden in his onscreen mailbox
Thomas ran Gremlin Net with distrust and the

network repaid him with LINE BUSY boxes and UNKNOWN RECIPIENT warnings whenever he tried to reach EARLYBIRDS, the Junior National Aeronautics and Space Administration contact address which Thomas tried most mornings, usually before school, after he'd checked his mailbox for emails from any NASA anoraks who may, or may not, have contacted him. Thomas was an anorak himself. He hunted NASA listings for COOLEST SITE THIS WEEK, hot goss from the NASA newsroom and updates on astronaut profiles. The life-stories of astronauts were a favourite with Thomas Moon. Not only, but partly, on account of his name, he'd wanted to be an astronaut for as long as he could remember.

It had started at primary school. Thomas could still remember the singsong rhythm of the names in Mr Smart's register. He would never forget them while he lived:

"Allborough?"

"Here, sir."

"Astley?"

"Here, sir."

"Butcher? Got any sausages?"

"No, sir, not today, sir."

"Dunbar? Elliott? Goulish?"

"Here, sir. Yes, sir. Here, sir."

"Feeling ghoulish, are we?"

"Yes sir, might be, sir."

"Kellog?"

"Yes, sir."

"Got your cornflakes, then?"

Jamie Kellog always giggled and reddened, even though Mr Smart said the same thing, in the same way, every morning register.

After Harriet Leeson and Abigail Massey, Mr Smart would reach:

"Mint?"

"Here, sir," Nicolas Mint would pipe up.

"Give me a Polo, would you?"

"Can't, sir, I ate them all up."

"Moon?"

"Here, sir," Thomas would say.

"Done any spacewalks lately?" Mr Smart would ask him. "Gone up in any rockets? Seen the man in the moon?"

"There isn't any man in the moon," Thomas would tell Mr Smart scornfully. "And one day, I'm going to go there."

Mr Smart would go on:

"Naylor?"

"Here, sir."

"Owen?"

"Here, sir."

"Make sure you put your spacesuit on, Thomas Moon," Mr Smart would joke over his glasses, before pressing on with Robertson, Saunders and Tancock. "You won't get far in space with your shirt hanging out of your trousers."

12

"Shouldn't you be going to school?"

Thomas Moon stared at the head that had suddenly appeared around his bedroom door. Its mouth opened and closed and said something he already knew.

"Shouldn't you be going to school?" his mother repeated.

"Oh. Yes. I'm going."

"What are you running now?" Thomas Moon's mother took a kindly interest in the screen. "Not trying to reach EARLYBIRDS again?"

"Um, yes, I am."

Thomas's mother sighed. "When are you going to spend as much time on schoolwork as you do on things about space?"

Um, Thomas felt, when pigs can fly? When spacemen call round for tea and give me a lift to Mission Control? When I get a place on the Young Astronauts Training Programme for the Millennium? When the earth runs out of spin, the sun runs out of shine, when Space Centre runs out of cash – that's when I'll spend time on schoolwork.

"The thing is, most astronauts study hard," Mrs Moon went on. "Most of them are chemists, biologists, physicists – that kind of thing."

This was true, Thomas had to admit. It said

so in Astronaut Profiles.

"It's silly to think about space travel, Tom, when you can't even concentrate in lessons."

"Maybe," Thomas said, grudgingly.

"You've got to come down to earth sometime. It's not very realistic."

"That's what they probably said to Columbus when he wanted to sail to America: it's not very *realistic*."

"But you're not Columbus, are you?"

"I've got plenty of time, Mum."

"You haven't – you're late already."

"For space, I mean. They need new people for space. And one day I'm going to get there."

And one day I'm going to GO there.

Two or three years passed after Mr Smart did the register and teased Thomas Moon about his name. Thomas Moon changed schools. He'd worked quite well for Mr Smart and for both the class teachers after him. But six months into secondary school, he decided to do no work. It didn't happen overnight. It happened as his interests changed and he saw that none of them coincided with what he was supposed to learn in school. Gradually he stopped trying to keep up. Grew more and more withdrawn. Started dreaming out of the window. Concerned at a thoroughly bad start, Thomas Moon's anxious parents switched him from Hubert Daley, the school where he'd started, to Boundary Road Community School, which was a bit farther away on the ring road; but still Thomas didn't work, and nothing changed at all except the windows Thomas looked out of.

Then the incredible happened. Aged eleven, as a snotty Year Seven, Thomas Moon met an astronaut. By chance he happened to be paying attention in Science on a day that changed the rest of his life. He could hardly believe his ears when Mr Frickers made the announcement:

"There is one place – and one place only – left on the Year Eight Science trip to the Royal Society Lecture. The lecture will take place at the University and will be given by Byron Hewitt, space-station astronaut. Will anyone wanting this place please – yes, Thomas Moon?"

"Please, Mr Frickers, yes please, sir." Thomas Moon's hand had shot up.

Mr Frickers pushed his spectacles further onto his nose. "I take it you'd like the place?"

"Yes please, Mr Frickers, I would."

"Any other takers?"

Amazingly – to Thomas Moon – there weren't. And so he got to go. As penance for being the only Year Seven on a Year Eight trip, he had to sit next to Mr Frickers on the coach and listen to Mr Frickers's views on Mr Quinlan. Mr Quinlan was head teacher at Boundary

15

Road Community School. A stickler for correctness in school uniform, he wrote long harangues in the school magazine about skirt length and acceptable trouser-colours, usually ending with a colourful simile likening failure to knot your tie correctly to setting a first foot on the Road to Ruin. Hardly ever stepping out of his office except to bark at someone, he knew no one – not even some of his staff – by name. He was either short-sighted or ignorant. Mr Frickers thought he knew which.

But the day had been too momentous to think about Quinlan. Thomas Moon had felt a rush of emotion the moment he entered the church-like University Hall, filled with the mutter and rustlings of Year Eights from twenty other schools, and saw Byron Hewitt up on stage in a grey zip-up suit with its exciting red zips and pockets and flaps and all his props around him. What, wondered Thomas Moon, could the balloon and the toy car be for? What about the teddy bear? Did they have bears in space?

When everyone had settled, Byron Hewitt was introduced. Then he began to speak in a thrillingly deep and informed voice that seemed to penetrate the very seat Thomas Moon was sitting in. Thomas Moon listened, agog, as Byron Hewitt explained that he had had to pass ninety-nine exams to qualify for training at Star City, in Moscow. Thomas tried to imagine *ninety-nine exams*, but failed to imagine passing them. He looked up. Byron Hewitt's thrillingly deep voice had moved on to rocket dynamics and was requesting volunteers.

"How do we move through space? Can we have a volunteer – someone from this side, please – "

Fifty arms wilted, Thomas Moon's among them, as Byron Hewitt selected someone from the opposite side of the Hall. The lucky volunteer skipped up onstage and held a balloon for Byron Hewitt. Byron Hewitt attached the blown-up balloon to a toy car. Then the volunteer released it, and the car shot across the stage. Thomas Moon leaned forward, gagging to see more, to be up there with Byron Hewitt, next to a *real* astronaut. Byron Hewitt held up the toy car. "What happened here?" he asked, immediately answering his own question before anyone else could. Air released suddenly *backwards* from the balloon, explained Byron Hewitt, propelled the toy car – he held up the car – *forwards*, thus demonstrating expulsion of gases, and therefore forward thrust, in a moving rocket. The volunteer skipped down again, to cheesy cheers from her mates.

The rest of the lecture washed by in a haze of facts and spinning figures for Thomas Moon. He didn't even hear Mr Frickers ask him what he thought, or react when Mr Frickers poked Helen Lacey for talking. Two more volunteers were requested, but Byron Hewitt's finger passed by Thomas Moon. At last, when the hour was almost up, Thomas Moon thought he might be lucky. But the last volunteer wasn't going to be him, after all, despite his straining arm saying *Me! Me! Me!* The last volunteer was the luckiest of all, and tried on Byron Hewitt's flight jacket. Flight suits were worn during missions, Hewitt explained. They had lots of zips and pockets with flaps to prevent things from floating out. After the final minutes of the video of his launch into space, and a ghostly tour through the space station, featuring Byron Hewitt's bedroom on Mir with the earth outside his window like a phosphorescent face peeping in, the lecture was over.

"You are the next generation of astronauts. One day," finished Byron Hewitt, "one of *you* will be in space."

And his arm had swung wide over his audience and his finger had seemed to point directly at Thomas Moon. Thomas Moon had queued up to meet him afterwards, though he could hardly remember it now. So overwhelmed had he been at the time, he could hardly remember anything Byron Hewitt had said to him personally, or almost anything about him, close up. But still he could remember the glow of meeting him, touching him, shaking his hand – *shaking the hand of an astronaut*.

That had been a while ago, now. Years and years had passed since Mr Smart had made a joke around Thomas Moon's name and first made him think about space, years in which nothing had changed except everything to do with space exploration and Thomas Moon's determination to be part of it. Now he was more determined than ever. He would join NASA's space team or die. First he'd train to be a pilot. That would be the best kind of start. Then he'd study like mad. At least, he *meant* to study like mad. Then he'd apply for the space programme. Most people he knew had raised an eyebrow. An astronaut? You're kidding. When are you going to grow up?

But Thomas Moon dared to dream. He'd be about the right age by the time the new International Space Station had had two or three years in orbit, just enough time to iron out any hiccups. Someone had to man it, why not Thomas Moon? Couldn't he at least *reach* for the stars, even if he couldn't catch them? And why not dream he could? If no one had ever dreamed they'd design a spaceship there'd never have *been* a space race; if no one looked up at the stars, no poets, explorers, astronomers, philosophers or sailors. Navigating by the stars was important, Thomas Moon knew. Helen Sharman said so.

Helen Sharman was an astronaut. Thomas had looked up Helen Sharman's website and learned that she became an astronaut by *hearing a plea for applicants over the radio*. Astronauts Wanted, it had said. No Experience Necessary. She'd only worked in a chocolate factory until she joined the programme to put a British astronaut in space. Then she'd had to learn Russian. Then she'd gone up in the Mir Space Station for *eight whole days* and done experiments, lucky duck. Thomas Moon burned to do the same. *Astronauts Wanted. No Experience Necessary.* But daydreaming got in the way. So did Gremlin Net.

...SORRY, LINE IS STILL BUSY... the screen announced.

Yeah, *right*. Impatiently Thomas shut down the computer, packed his bag for school and left the house for the bus stop. He would try again tonight. He couldn't let the Gremlin Net block his attempts to catch EARLYBIRDS. What did it think, it could *win*?

DO YOU MEAN ME?

Here's Mister Spaceman dreaming out of the window … of all the things he could become …

"Thomas! Thomas Moon!"

Whatever Mister Spaceman dreams comes true … he only has to dream it… Thomas Moon stared out of the classroom window from the topmost floor of Main Block. Out on the school playing fields distant figures picked up balls and milled around and did things. Up on the furthest pitch, a one-sided game of hockey neared half-time. Behind the playing fields dozed the town, and beyond the town a skyful of regular clouds drifted by. Thomas wished he were out there under the clouds. Anywhere but here. *I'm not here, I'm there,* he told himself. *I'm not here, I'm there. I'm up and away, I am.*

"Thomas Moon! Eyes front!"

Thomas Moon pictured himself walking out

onto the field and through the game of hockey, mounting over the fluffy tops of the trees and onto the clouds and up and away into space. He'd just walk right up into the sky, because he *could*. Soon he'd be world-famous for being able to breathe in airless atmospheres and flying in space unaided. The French would request that he relaunch the failed Ariane mission. Mission Control at Houston would ask him to check out the shuttle as a courtesy gesture. He'd make a fortune checking satellite communications and Global Positioning systems...

"Thomas Moon! Can you hear me?"

How would he feel if he saw a spaceman *right now*, bouncing across the playing field with the sun glinting fiercely off his Extra-Vehicular Activity suit? How would he feel if that spaceman stopped and waved? Thomas imagined things he might ask him. *Is it tough to walk in that suit? I'm a space cadet too, right? School? Just a simulation. I'll be in space someday, too. Where did you land from? Where are you going? Will you take me with you?* And the spaceman would nod with Main Block at school reflected in his blank black visor, where a spaceman's face ought to be.

If *he* were a spaceman himself, Thomas thought, he'd come back and visit people at school for a laugh and show them his space-boots and tubes of old space food and pictures of the earth glowing in space like nothing you ever saw and bring bits of spacecraft along. He might even show them experiments. He'd power-pack down over the playing fields one day, after Quinlan – that's *Mister Head Teacher* Quinlan – had agreed to pay him a fee of five hundred pounds, or probably five thousand, and he'd look down, and there'd be the trees, the town, the school. He'd even look down on Quinlan's office. Probably he'd land on it, somehow. The day he came back to sign autographs, probably he'd—

"What's so interesting about the window?"

"I'm sorry?" Thomas started.

"You. Thomas Moon." Mrs Jasper looked at him coldly. "I've been calling your name for the last five minutes. What have we just been saying about Oliver Cromwell?"

"He made a model army?" Thomas hazarded. "He had a big wart on his face?"

"And?"

"I don't know. I'm sorry."

Mrs Jasper brought her face close to Thomas's. A strong smell of horses rose from her slubby jumper.

"What's so interesting about the window?" she asked him again.

I'm not here, I'm there.

"Um, nothing, miss." Thomas shrugged.

Mrs Jasper looked at him. "You can do better than this."

Thomas flushed. "I'm sorry."

Mrs Jasper pursed her lips.

"Pick up your books. Eleanor, would you mind moving? Come on, Thomas – front row."

Thomas Moon rose wearily. He was used to the front row these days. Mr Samuels kept him under his nose for Maths, Mrs Easterhouse practically ate him whole for English, and even Miss Johns had moved him, apologetically, for Geography. *A dreamer*, they wrote on his reports. *Thomas has allowed his attention to wander this term*. Easter term, summer term, winter term. Nearly always the reports said the same.

Thomas was hardened to comments like these. Except for reading during French, he didn't regret a thing. Reading a book about space flight in Mrs Carrier's French lesson had been the one thing he wished he hadn't done. He'd always liked Mrs Carrier. Louise Carrier had a very nice smile, and she fixed it on Thomas quite a lot. She had a theory about Thomas. Her theory was, he'd respond to extra attention. He did respond, of course, but still – something vital was missing. Some confidence. Some key. Other teachers had given him up as a hopeless non-achiever. But Mrs Carrier had always – up until the day he betrayed her – had time for Thomas Moon.

The day Thomas Moon betrayed Mrs Carrier's trust in him, the day he hadn't been able to put down *Mir: A History of Space Stations* and had sat at the back of the class and jammed his French reader around it, had probably been the day he'd take back if he could have his life over again.

It had worked all right to start with. So long as he looked attentive, he found he could read pretty well. If he looked up now and again, nodded and mouthed with the rest of the class and met Mrs Carrier's eyes, he could get away with it easily. But soon he'd got engrossed. He forgot to look up. Forgot to nod. Forgot everything but the delays the core station had suffered and the preparation of Associated Modules. He didn't see everyone else turning to *La Famille Delarge*, the exercise he should have been studying. He didn't see Barry or Mint or Tedious or any of his other friends staring. He didn't hear Rebby Elwares sniggering or Mrs Carrier clearing her throat. He didn't hear anything at all except the thrust and burn of space stations manoeuvring in space where, in reality, you wouldn't hear a thing.

Reality soon broke over Thomas Moon. Still speaking, Mrs Carrier fixed her eyes on the top of Thomas's head and made her way down the room. Closer and closer she came, willing him to be deep in his French. Still Thomas didn't look up. Mrs Carrier actually felt tears springing into her eyes when she saw that he was reading a book – any book – how could he?

"Tom – how *could* you?" The look on her face showed how hurt she was. "After *all* the work we've been doing."

"I'm sorry, I've got to take it back soon, I—"

"Never mind excuses." Mrs Carrier whisked away the book. In a hard voice she said: "Down to the front of the class, please."

Something had gone out of Mrs Carrier after that. She went back to the front of the class and stowed *Mir: A History of Space Stations* in her desk. She didn't say anything else. But from that moment on, she never smiled at Thomas Moon or gave him her extra attention. After the lesson Thomas came to her and tried to explain that he *did* like French, it was just that he liked space travel *more*. Maybe they could do something about space travel *in* French? Or whatever Mrs Carrier wanted? He wouldn't do it again. He hadn't *meant* to do it today, it had just kind of … happened.

Mrs Carrier had listened, more in sorrow than in anger. After Thomas had gone she looked at his book. French adverbs and the adventures of *La Famille Delarge*, she could see, had nothing on correctional thrusters and booster burns in space or a spot of EVA (Extra-Vehicular Activity) with an MMU

(Manned Manoeuvring Unit). She remembered his expression. Thomas Moon had been *way* up in space when she'd snatched away his book. Instead of the numberless stars winking behind him and the luminous earth below him and a job of welding to be done in the glare of the merciless space-sun, she'd brought him back to earth with a jolt, leaving him sitting in French with a flushed-looking face and no way to hide what he'd been doing. After all they *had* been doing. Mrs Carrier sighed. She'd thought they'd been making progress. But at least she understood now. Her efforts – and French adverbs – simply didn't exist for Thomas Moon.

He'd let Mrs Carrier down badly, Thomas Moon knew. He desperately wished he hadn't. He'd take it back if he could. Mrs Carrier thought he was rubbish now, Thomas could see. *He would have to learn what she wanted him to learn* to get back in favour now, but that was a call too far for Thomas Moon. He had his own agenda. He could no more change his heart than change his eyes.

He closed his eyes and wished that lesson away. It had been the first of many moves to the front of the class, so Mrs Jasper hadn't *got* to him that morning. Not the way Mrs Carrier had. Thomas had got used to it by now. Mrs Jasper had moved him before. He'd only just worked his way back.

"You wouldn't think she only just moved you," Nicolas Mint observed over lunch in the noisy canteen. "She's only got to move you *again*."

Thomas Moon shrugged. He didn't want to talk about it.

"Now she can spit all over you, right? Pity she smells of horses."

Mrs Jasper kept horses and smelled of them, everyone knew. She also looked astonishingly like Oliver Cromwell.

"Probably you'll smell of 'em too," Mint finished, dolefully. "Now she's got you in front with all the sad people."

Thomas Moon ignored him. His thoughts were fully on space food. American astronauts, he knew, could breakfast on peaches or bran-flakes, ham or scrambled eggs. They could lunch on frankfurters, peanuts and asparagus, or have shrimp cocktail, beef with barbecue sauce, green beans, mushrooms and strawberries for dinner. It was pretty sophisticated, these days. Clever, the way they'd thought it out. Especially the re-use of water.

"Water's recycled from the toilet," he said. "It's clever, see? That way, none gets wasted."

"Excuse me?" Mint rolled his eyes.

"In spacecraft," Thomas explained, "the toilet's like a funnel with these footstraps, else you'd float away? They collect urine and filter it, then they evaporate water from your wee.

28

And the food – it's mainly dried or tinned, but really good these days. You can actually go for *six days* without eating the same thing twice."

"Or drinking your own wee."

"Fun city," put in Tedious. "Why not sit in a lift with a Pot Noodle instead?"

"I do," said Thomas Moon.

Philip Tettios – called Tedious – didn't know how to take this. In the end he said, "I'm getting pudding."

Returning five minutes later with some mess covered in custard, he found Thomas Moon deep in thought. Space food, Thomas knew, was carefully, nutritionally designed. Not at all like school dinners. School dinners were designed by someone who thought people would *go* for cauliflower cheese. Thomas was personally prepared to go quite a way to *avoid* cauliflower cheese, into space if he had to. Cauliflower cheese would be a nightmare in space. But at least you wouldn't have to smell it.

"There's no smells in space," he suddenly said.

"Do what?"

"No smells," Thomas said. "No fresh air."

Mint rolled his eyes again. "You're going to tell me why."

"All air is filtered to remove dead skin cells and debris, plus it's recycled chemically and pumped round the system to —"

"You mean, you can't smell food?"

Thomas shook his head. "I told you, all air's filtered. Plus everything comes in containers and you suck it up through straws." He picked up a chip. "If we were in space now I could just *throw* this towards your mouth and it would just drift across and go in."

"Cool."

"Plus you can feel food floating around in your stomach? Until it gets to your intestines. Then your muscles push it through."

"What if your intestines float as well?"

"They do."

"I'd throw up my guts if they floated."

"You'd have to throw up in a bag, or there'd be blobs of sick in the air and they'd get in the filters."

"Gross." Mint thought about it.

"I found this email the other day – " Biting the corner off a triangle of processed cheese, which was as near to vacuum-packed space food as he could get, Thomas Moon squeezed it into his mouth. " – bundled with something else on Gremlin Net? D'you wonder where things come from? I mean, they *could* come from anywhere. Someone might profile your visits to certain websites – collecting 'cookies' it's called, when they pick up a trace – and recruit you for going into space or something, and start to send you emails –"

"They might," Tedious said. "In Fantasy

30

Land."

"Gremlin what?" Mint said.

"Don't you have email?"

"I have," Tedious volunteered. "I never heard of that server."

"Does it foul up for you sometimes?"

"It does me," Mint said. "It's always busy when I try. Plus I've got no one to email."

"Gremlin Net hates me," Thomas said. "I *know* it loses mail."

"How can it?" Tedious wondered. "You only have to click SEND."

"Even if I do it step by step, it still stuffs up on me sometimes. But it *better not* stuff up tonight." Thomas's eyes took on a faraway look as he thought of a message, a very *particular* message, he possibly might send that night.

"Thomas Moon!" Mint put on his Mrs Jasper voice. "Thomas Moon! Eyes front!"

Tedious sniggered.

But Thomas was still in the clouds.

"When I go up in space," he said, "I'm going to take a diary and write down what I *feel*."

Mint regarded him affectionately.

"As if they'd want *you* up in space, you dopey man-in-the-moon."

Thomas Moon threw a chip at Nicolas Mint. Mint, who understood him so well. The Mint he'd been to *primary* school with, can you believe, and never really noticed for some reason. Thomas had swapped schools a lot since then, ending up at Boundary Road Community School some two years ago, to find a dimly remembered Nicolas Mint kind of *waiting* for him. They'd shared a lot since then. But they hadn't shared Golding's Hotel.

Thomas Moon's way home that night lay past Golding's Hotel. He *almost* took the steps up to the gilded glass doors, then changed his mind and didn't. Golding's Hotel, the best hotel in town, was part – an important part – of Thomas Moon's Training Programme, along with the Gun Room Gym.

Physical fitness was paramount. That's what Irving Graham, rookie astronaut, had said, back in the Earlybirds Reach for the Stars Aspirational Contacts listings. Tom wasn't at all sure what paramount meant, but it had to mean that fitness was favourite. And he meant to keep in tiptop shape. He'd been simulating training conditions for some time now. Golding's Hotel came into it. But it wouldn't come into it tonight.

Tonight he had a date with the Gremlin. And it better not act up this time. Thomas Moon hurried home. Ignoring the smell of paint filling the house, he flung himself into his bedroom and ripped off his sweater and tie.

Thomas switched on the computer.

FOUND CDROM the screen winked.

Clicking on SHORTCUT TO GREMLIN NET,

then CONNECT, Thomas waited. He felt cool and fatalistic.

BEEE – WHEEE – DIM-DUM-DI-DUM – the familiar screech reminded him that the Net was there to serve him.

This time he got a connection.

Opening "Pandora" and selecting MESSAGE /NEW MESSAGE, RECIPIENT EARLYBIRDS, he began to type:

```
Return-Path: <Thomas.Moon@gremlin.net
From: Thomas<Thomas.Moon@gremlin.net
To: Earlybirds.@earlybirds.nas.ac.us
Date: Tue 4 Apr 15:45:28 GMTOBST
Subject: Recruits!
Hey, Earlybirds, I just read your
webpage, cool! Please tell me
MORE, MORE, MORE about candidate
astronaut status! How do I apply?
Over,
Thomas Moon
```

Was that all? He guessed so.

Thomas clicked SEND and the message went out over the wires to begin his new life, the very first secret step. Many years later he would coolly say, "I guess it began with Gremlin Net ... or not."

Flushed with success, he went to check his mail.

YOU HAVE NEW MAIL! The usual box told

him, bursting with congratulations. Double
clicking on the newly listed incoming message,
Thomas read eagerly:

```
Return-Path: <Earlybirds@
earlybirds.nas.ac.us
From: Earlybirds<Earlybirds@
earlybirds.nas.ac.us
To: Thomas.Moon@gremlin.net
Date: Tue 4 Apr 09:15:18 GMTOBST
Subject: The Right Stuff
Dear Thomas Moon,
Re: Recruits!
Any adult man or woman in excellent
physical condition who meets the
basic qualifications can be selec-
ted to enter astronaut training.
Mission specialists and pilots
will need a degree in engineering,
science or mathematics, plus three
years of related experience.
Pilots need good vision! If you
have at least a thousand hours'
air-time in a jet aircraft, you
will still be competing with over
4,000 applicants for every 20
astronaut openings every two
years. For more on astronaut
training, page our Fact Sheets.
Good Luck!
Mission Control
```

This was a total puzzler. Thomas began to wonder what he'd just done. Hadn't he only just sent out a message – *yet here was its answer*, not two seconds after he'd sent it? Wait – the message was dated this morning:

```
Date: Tue 4 Apr 09:15:18 GMTOBST
```

So some bright Earlybird had sent him what he needed to know about a quarter of an hour after *he'd failed to get through this morning and left the house*. Weird. Psychic. Nice one. And there was something else. Right at the bottom of the screen, it said:

```
"Text_2.TXT" Attached.
```

Thomas's brain tingled. *This was what had happened the last time*. When he'd found the other message, mysteriously bundled under a text file.

Rapidly making a search for a text file named Text_2.TXT, Thomas scrolled through hidden lists, then highlighted, clicked and held his breath. Just like it had the last time, the hidden message popped up:

```
Return-Path: <SPM29@starlight.ac.uk
From: SPM29@starlight.ac.uk
To: Thomas.Moon@gremlin.net
Date: Tue 4 Apr 09:15:18 GMTOBST
Subject: It Could Be You
```

```
Content-Type: text/plain
Content-Description: Text_2
Content-Disposition: attachment
filename="Text_2.TXT"
Attachment Converted:
C:\COMMS\PANDORA\Text_14.TXT
CALLING ALL VOLUNTEERS
T MINUS TWELVE WEEKS
LIFT-OFF 4th JULY
CONGRATULATIONS!
YOUR SELECTION FOR ASTRONAUT
STATUS
PROCESSED WITH CODE WORD
"COLUMBUS".
PLEASE CONFIRM.
OVER.
MISTER SPACEMAN
```

SPM 29 again! This time *from* Mister Spaceman! How many Mister Spacemen *were*
there? Thomas Moon frowned. Astronauts
never allowed themselves to be flustered
by incoming information. He'd better think
it out. It had been sent at 9:15 today. Where
had it come from? The message couldn't
be clearer:

```
CONGRATULATIONS! YOUR SELECTION
FOR ASTRONAUT STATUS PROCESSED
WITH CODE WORD "COLUMBUS".
```

Calling all volunteers. Congratulations! Celebrations! It was real. Tom looked at himself in the mirror. It was just like Helen Sharman hearing it over the radio. Astronaut Wanted – No Experience Necessary. The call – the call had come. Maybe they were recruiting young for the post-millennial Programme. Maybe enthusiasm counted. Maybe they knew who he was. Thomas gripped the mouse. Unbelievably, it was *that* easy. To be accepted for astronaut training and realize his wildest dreams, all he had to do was SEND the coded return.

"Tom! Is that you?" his mother called from the living-room.

"No, it's Dale Winton, who did you think?" Thomas Moon typed swiftly.

"I thought I heard you up there! Come and look at this!"

"Not now, Mum, I'm busy."

Thomas typed swifter still.

"Thomas! Are you there?"

Thomas reread his message:

```
Return-Path: <Thomas.Moon@gremlin.net
From: Thomas<Thomas.Moon@gremlin.net
To: SPM29@starlight.ac.uk
Date: Tue 4 Apr 15:49:00 GMTOBST
Subject: Sign Me Up

COLUMBUS*COLUMBUS*COLUMBUS*COLUM-
BUS*COLUMBUS*COLUMBUS*COLUMBUS*COL
```

```
UMBUS*COLUMBUS*COLUMBUS*COLUMBUS*C
OLUMBUS*COLUMBUS*COLUMBUS*COLUM—
BUS*COLUMBUS*COLUMBUS*COLUMBUS*COL
UMBUS*COLUMBUS*COLUMBUS*COLUMBUS*C
OLUMBUS*COLUMBUS*COLUMBUS*COLUM—
BUS*COLUMBUS*COLUMBUS*COLUMBUS*COL
UMBUS*COLUMBUS*COLUMBUS*COLUMBUS*C
OLUMBUS*COLUMBUS*COLUMBUS*COLUM—
BUS*COLUMBUS*COLUMBUS*COLUMBUS*COL
UMBUS*COLUMBUS*COLUMBUS*COLUMBUS*C
OLUMBUS*COLUMBUS*COLUMBUS*COLUMBUS
OVER
THOMAS COLIN MOON
```

Thomas pressed SEND. The screenful of COLUMBUSes winged its way down the phone lines saying, YES, YES, YES, YES, *YES*. COUNT ME IN. ROGER. CHECK. AFFIRMATIVE. YOUR SPACEMAN.

"Tom?"

"Yes?"

"I'm waiting. Come and see what I've done!"

Thomas Moon sat back. It felt good, really good, to see those COLUMBUSes sailing away. *We copy your message and accept your mission. T minus twelve weeks exactly*. One small step for man, one *giant* step for Thomas Moon. How exciting was *that*? His first real step into uncharted space and utter solitude...

"You know those wires in the living-room?"

38

Mrs Moon's voice went on. "I've painted over them – won't matter, will it? What d'you think of this blue – I'm doing the hall tomorrow!"

On her half-day, probably. Thomas Moon's heart sank. As a busy businesswoman with her own card and gift shop, his mother didn't get a lot of time for decorating. But Wednesday half-day was always a flashpoint, he knew. She had only to sight a pot of paint and she was off – painting over anything that couldn't pack up its bags and crawl away.

"Yes, all right – I'm coming!"

With a backward glance at the interlocked-rockets screen saver that winked away as the computer shut down, Thomas Moon –

CONGRATULATIONS! AND CELEBRATIONS!

I WANT THE WORLD TO KNOW HOW HAPPY I CAN BE!

– *Young astronaut candidate – Mister Spaceman – clumped through the house to view the painted-over wires in the living-room.*

CALLING ALL VOLUNTEERS

Thomas Moon's Training and Exercise Programme was strict but simple. It didn't interfere, hardly at all, with his mother's life, or his father's. They could simply get on with whatever they were doing, and Thomas would get on with *his* life. His father was absent on business – World of Cladding business – more often than he was at home, in any case, so nothing would interfere with *that*. World of Cladding was a demanding employer. Mr Moon's firm regularly sent him to Dublin, Derby, Doncaster and Droitwich on business, everywhere beginning with a *D*, it seemed, where Exterior Cladding for Home and Business – Thomas was still pretty vague about what it was – seemed to be top of their wish list. Mr Moon lived in hopes of a business trip to Dubai, Dar es Salaam, Dallas, Darjeeling, Djibouti or Djakarta. But all he got was Droitwich.

Thomas Moon's mother had other things on her mind. Business at the shop wasn't going too well. Plus the house was filthy, she knew it. Nothing a lick of paint wouldn't fix. Wednesday half-day would do it.

Thomas Moon steered clear. He wasn't about to get involved in a major paint-down of the house. Nothing must interfere with his Training and Exercise Programme. Not even Nicolas Mint moving away.

"Oh, *what*?" he'd said, when he heard. "Don't move away, Mint – you *can't*."

"I can't not," Mint said, as miserable as he was.

Mint mumbled something about Tom coming to visit, but they both knew it was the end. Thomas felt the spaces passing between them. He felt absolutely gutted. They'd been through a lot together over the years. Now miles of motorway would come between them. It had to force them apart.

"Where *is* Ludlow, anyhow?" he asked, at last. It sounded like an American football player or something. Ludlow Flinks for the Fliers.

"Somewhere in Shropshire, I think," Mint told him glumly.

"Where's Shropshire?"

"Somewhere near Wales. I dunno."

"Do you *have* to go?"

"Dad's job."

"Right."

41

There was nothing else to be said. But the surface of Thomas Moon's home planet had wrinkled considerably. His school years would be different, minus Mint. How many best mates *had* he, that he could afford to lose one to stupid Ludlow, Shropshire?

To forget about Mint, or the soon-to-be *absence* of Mint-like body particles, Thomas Moon intensified his Training Programme. The Training Programme mimicked a Mission Specialist's as closely as Thomas was able. Mission Specialists were the only crew-members to do EVAs, or spacewalks, operate the remote manipulator system, do specific experiment operations – and who wanted to do anything *else*?

It meant he had to be ready. It also meant that he had to grow – to a minimum of 163 centimetres, preferably 193. Now that the recruitment call had come, probably from British sponsors of a future collaborative mission, he had to be on stand-by, didn't he?

Soon he would find out more. Soon they would tell him how he could prepare for his future entry to the space programme. Study, work, train, learn all you can about space. It couldn't be so different from what he was doing already, except for the studying part. The message had mentioned *lift-off*, 4th July. How exciting was *that*?

*　　*　　*

Despite Thomas begging him not to, Mint moved away in May. Thomas's first email to Mint let Mint know he hadn't forgiven him:

```
Return-Path: <Thomas.Moon@gremlin.net
From: TCM24<Thomas.Moon@gremlin.net
To: Mint@Mint.ogre.co.uk
Date: Wed 27 May 08:11:21 GMTOBST
Subject: Suffer, You Moron
Mint,
Hope you hate Ludlow.
Hope everything goes wrong so you
pack up and come back straight
away. School stinks as usual,
school trip today to The Merchant
of Venice, can't wait. I'm train-
ing like mad and keeping in shape.
I'm doing more work in Chemistry,
but Frensham, he doesn't even
notice. He only told me the other
day I shouldn't ask questions in
class. He goes, Moon, we're hon-
oured you're with us. Moon, stop
playing the clown. I don't care
what Frensham says, I need to get
good in chemistry. It's listed for
Mission Specialists. How else am I
going to EVA?
Mum just painted the living-room
blue. She painted over the telly
wires, light switches, everything.
```

She painted the kitchen once,
there was this calendar on the
wall, and she even painted over
that. She's always in too much of
a hurry, Dad says. He was wicked
off she painted the lights blue.
She even painted the table blue.
She painted everything. Then she
goes, I've ordered a carpet. What
colour is it? Blue, of course.
Coming Tuesday, like it or lump
it. So then we can't wear shoes.
Got to go now. Hope I manage to
send this. Neil sits where you sit
in maths. We don't even notice the
difference, except there's no
smell. Guess what, I got selected
for Astronaut Status! An email
from someone called Spaceman!
Wish you hadn't moved away.
Smell you later,
Moon

Thomas clicked SEND and went to school.
The Gremlin was eating out of his hand these
days. He just about had it gripped. But still, he
missed Mint. More than he cared to admit.

*   *   *

The school trip to the theatre had lift-off at one o'clock. Everyone had boarded the bus tumultuously after lunch. After they'd all decanted themselves, noisily, off the coach onto the rain-darkened pavement outside the Palace Theatre, and had all trooped in under the red plastic capitals announcing

TODAY AND FOR A FOUR WEEK SEASON
THE SOUTHERN SHAKESPEARE COMPANY PRESENTS
MARCIA STRICKLAND, CELIA WEXFORD,
DANIEL JAMIESON, PETER GATES IN
THE MERCHANT OF VENICE

they milled around in the foyer, wishing it were a film or a band or anything but a Shakespeare play they were going to have to sit through.

Thomas Moon had been reading *The Merchant of Venice* in class, under Mrs Easterhouse's eagle eye. Maybe he missed something somewhere, but he still didn't really understand – he didn't think he ever would – why Shylock wanted a pound of Antonio's flesh. It wouldn't make up for the money Antonio owed him. All it would do was make a mess. The scene where Portia begged him not to do it was still the best bit in the play. The rest was pretty dull, to tell the truth. Maybe it would've been better, Thomas thought, if either *more* people had wanted pounds of flesh, or maybe if everybody did – except Portia, who

45

wouldn't – or maybe if *nobody* did. It was a pretty gruesome idea, even for Will "Is-this-a-knife-I-see-before-me" Shakespeare.

After they'd stocked up with programmes and Ribena, the only drink on offer, plus wine gums and Starburst and mint imperials, and had trooped into the old-fashioned plush-seated auditorium where Barry and Tedious were hamming it up already and pretending to fall over seats, and had been *shown* into their seats by a not-very-pleased usherette, already Thomas Moon was wishing he could sit somewhere else. Tedious and Barry and Neil were OK sometimes, but today he wasn't in the mood. He wasn't in the mood because – surprise – he wouldn't mind watching the play. Mint would have understood. Mint had taste. Plus, he wasn't stupid.

Tedious and Barry and Neil were stupid. After a while, despite his awe when the curtain went up on Antonio and his mates – most of them dressed in red velvet and looking much older than he'd thought – Thomas Moon got infected with stupid, himself. *Stupid* seemed to run up the row of seats like a thrill of electric current. Once he started laughing, he found he couldn't stop.

"Do you *mind*?" The woman sitting in front of him turned to glare at Thomas Moon.

Thomas looked blank. "Sorry." Then he mugged "Do-you-mind?" up the row, which made things so much better – ha – he could hardly *look* at Tedious.

He tried hard, he really did, to concentrate on the play. When old Gobbo came on, he looked straight ahead and tried to keep a straight face. As it went, old Gobbo didn't have much to do with the action, so Thomas wasn't too grieved when he went off-stage with a basket.

Suddenly something hit him. He looked up the row and copped one in the face – a mint imperial, no less. He chucked a few back and missed. *You prat*, he mouthed up at Neil. Neil grinned and threw two more, one hitting someone next to, or possibly actually hitting, the woman in front of Thomas Moon. The woman flinched. She suddenly turned and torched him with her eyes. "Can you stop *doing* that, please."

Thomas Moon shrank in his seat.

"Well," Shylock was saying, "thou shalt see; thy eyes shall be thy judge, the difference of old Shylock and Bassanio."

Barry had produced a coin and was quietly unscrewing a cruddy old ashtray off the back of the seat in front of him. Thomas Moon was scandalized. *You can't do that!* he signalled. Then he produced a coin himself, and slowly, with exaggerated caution and much gurning at the back of her head, he began unscrewing the ashtray behind the complainer. She might turn at any moment. How thrilling it was, how *dangerous* – almost as dangerous as old Antonio's potential flesh-removal situation. With quick and nervous fingers, Thomas worked. An evil genie had got into him. He didn't know what he was doing.

He just about had the ashtray unscrewed when a hail of mint imperials strafed his head. He felt the rebound in the seat as the woman in front sprang up. Mint imperials rattled off her and rolled about on the floor. *"Really!"* she said, "this is *too* much!" The person next to her turned around and gave them an ugly stare.

It was over the top, Thomas knew. He was about to hiss "Pack it in" down the row to Neil, except that Neil was killing himself laughing, when the woman in front abruptly excused herself and went out.

Thomas soon forgot her. Soon he was absorbed in the play. They'd finally almost got to the bit when Portia gives it the old "The quality of mercy is not strained, it droppeth as the gentle rain from heaven upon the place beneath," when he noticed Mrs Easterhouse imperiously gesturing someone out. What – *me*? Thomas Moon fingered his chest. Yes, *you* her finger gestured. You – Thomas Moon – out *now*.

The whole row got up to let them go – Moonie, Barry, Tedious and Neil – in that order. In that order, Mrs Easterhouse ranged them in the foyer. She looked at them coldly, then hotly. Spots of rage stood in her cheeks.

"I've just had the pleasure," she said furiously, "of assuring a member of the public that she'll be able to watch the remainder of this play undisturbed. I've never been so embarrassed. I didn't know what to say." She swept them all with a look which had quite a *lot* to say. "Would anyone like to tell me what may have disturbed the lady who complained to me? Philip – any ideas?"

"We were laughing a bit," said Tedious. "Probably that's what it was."

"And?" Mrs Easterhouse waited. A small vein ticked in her neck.

"Tom wanted a mint, so I chucked him one," Neil added, in a small voice. "Only one or two," he said, smaller still.

Thomas had an ashtray in his pocket. Behind the double doors to the theatre and the stage, he could hear his favourite scene, the courtroom scene, unfolding in all its drama and its pathos. He felt cross with himself for being involved. He wished Mrs Easterhouse would get on with it. Then they could go back in and catch what was left of the play.

"And *you*, Thomas –" Mrs Easterhouse fell on Thomas Moon "– *you* of all people. I thought you *enjoyed* the play in class."

Thomas looked up, surprised. "I did, I—"

"So you thought you'd come to the theatre and spoil it for someone else. You don't deserve – none of you –" Mrs Easterhouse let them have it "– you don't deserve to come on a school trip *ever again*! Sit down there and don't let me hear you say a *word*."

After they'd sat a quarter of an hour or so in tense silence in the foyer, Thomas realized, with growing hurt and amazement, that they weren't going to be allowed back into the theatre to see the rest of the play. They hadn't meant any harm, surely Mrs Easterhouse could see? Couldn't they go back in and just say sorry? He could hear the play going on and felt quite desperate. He hadn't realized, until now, just how much he'd wanted to see it.

He felt quite upset by the end. The burble and blurt of the unfolding drama rose and fell behind the double doors. The final storm of applause at the end made it pretty hard to swallow. He'd missed it all, the whole play, but he supposed he could see the justice.

At last the play spilled out. Laughing and chattering to start with, most people fell suddenly quiet on filing past them. As if they were lepers or something, Thomas thought. Finally the foyer cleared and they were allowed to get onto the coach, each of them next to a teacher, each of them thoroughly quashed. How much worse can it get, said Neil's expression.

In the event, it got a lot worse. Far from the

whole thing being over, it had only just begun. Mrs Easterhouse had had plenty of time on the coach trip back to school to work herself up into a towering rage of indignation. She gave Head of English both barrels as soon as she found him.

Head of English summoned them in. The dressing-down he gave them practically stripped the paint off the walls and withered the plants on his desk. The worst bit was when he softened, near the end.

"I thought you *liked* English, Thomas."

"I do. I like English a lot."

Head of English looked at him. "Well," he sighed, "I give up. Mrs Carrier always sticks up for you, you know. But I think this proves her wrong at last, don't you?"

Thomas nodded miserably, ready to agree with anything.

"I'm sending you to Mr Quinlan." Head of English got up coolly. "We'll see what *he* has to say."

Oh, *what*? Thomas blinked. Quinlan as *well*? On *top* of everything else? A kind of resentment set in, in the corridor outside Quinlan's office. He'd been punished enough, Thomas knew. It was right that they'd missed the rest of the play. Old Easterhouse had given them hell, and they were probably up for that, too. But after that it got silly. It was getting sillier, now.

51

One by one, they saw Mr Quinlan in his office. Tedious came out in tears. Thomas was last to go in.

He didn't actually hear a lot of what Mr Quinlan said, because the caretaker, Mr Sumner, was noisily strimming the grass outside Mr Quinlan's office window.

"Disturbing reports ..." *ZEE-WHEE-ZEE* "that a *member of the public* should..." *ZEE-ZEE-ZEE* "Mrs Easterhouse informs me you ..." *ZAZZ-ZEE* "uniform, you *represent the school* ... is this the way you *normally –*" *ZEE-MEE-WHEE –*

"I'm sorry," Thomas mumbled, in response, he thought, to what Mr Quinlan wanted.

"When in uniform you *are*" – *ZEE-WHEE* "– an example will have to be made ..." *ZIZZZ-MIZZZ* "... shocked that this should ..." *ZAZZ-BZAZZ-MAZZ –*

Mr Sumner's strimmer took on a desperate high note. *ZAZ-ZIZZ-ZIZZ-ZIZZ* – Clumps of something mud-like hit the window and spattered all over Mr Sumner. Thomas watched, fascinated, as Mr Sumner, swearing loudly, flung down his strimmer and backed away in disgust.

Crossing swiftly to the window, Quinlan threw it open. "Mr Sumner, I take it you're finishing now?"

"I am now I hit some dog-do." Mr Sumner looked down at his shirt and trousers in disbelief. The effect of a moment's inattention had been quite astonishing. He looked as if he'd been shot-blasted with poo. He actually had it on his *face*.

"Thank you, Mr Sumner."

Mr Quinlan humourlessly screwed up the window and returned to Thomas Moon. "As I was saying, you've let the school down badly. *To think* that a pupil from Boundary Road Community School –" Quinlan puffed up with indignation "–to *think* that a Boundary Road pupil *privileged to go on a school trip* should –"

"I know, Mr Quinlan, I'm sorry."

"When you are out in uniform, you are the public face of the school. You do not eat at the bus stop. You give up your seat on buses. You behave impeccably on school trips, when you represent the school –"

Thomas began to drift off. Mr Sumner's display outside had made him curious to see it repeated. Strimming through dog poo seemed to produce some pretty dramatic results. Would cat poo do, as well? Perhaps he could arrange an accident-in-waiting for someone else, sometime – but who did he hate that much?

"This isn't the first time you've shown a complete disregard for the feelings of others. Life, you know Thomas, is like a bicycle. Pedal fast, you can get a long way. But you *can't ride over other people.*"

Quinlan was winding down, Thomas knew. He was fond of wrapping things up with peculiar sayings which he thought were pithy and clever – "Life is like a bicycle" was a favourite – which in fact left people who didn't know him with the impression that he was on mind-bending drugs. Thomas had missed whole tracts of what he'd said, but he guessed he could join the dots. He looked Quinlan straight in the eye with dislike. He hadn't bothered to find out how Thomas felt, and how bad – or not – it *really* was. He'd simply taken the easiest course, and brought out the heavy guns. From that moment on, Thomas had trouble receiving him. It seemed the line had static. Satellite communications were down. Moon orbit interfered with transmission. Or something. Over and out.

"Thomas – did you hear what I said?"

"No, Mr Quinlan. I mean, yes, Mr Quinlan."

"This isn't the first time, Thomas. And in this case, I must insist."

"Yes, Mr Quinlan." On what?

"You're suspended," Mr Quinlan finished. "As from now."

Tedious lifted his bleary face when Thomas joined him in the corridor.

"Suspended?"

"Yeah."

"Me, too."

"He's ringing my parents."

"And mine."

After Thomas's parents had been summoned to see Mr Quinlan later that day after school, and Thomas had gone dolefully home with them afterwards, nothing much more was said.

But that evening, when his mother looked up from her weekly accounts and Thomas looked up and found her eyes resting on him and knew she was really upset, Thomas Moon shrugged and said, "Don't worry, Mum. It's only Quinlan."

"Of *course* I worry."

"There's no point."

"Yes, there is."

"It's a school rules thing. They don't listen. It doesn't matter what you say."

"Why are you *doing* this?"

"What?"

"*This* – why can't you do as you're told?"

"I don't know," Thomas said. But something in his chest *did* know. Something in his chest would burst before it gave in. "What was really stupid, was –" Thomas felt ready to cry "– I wanted to see the play, and I couldn't. That's what was really stupid."

Thomas's mother got up and hugged him.

"Never you mind," she said, "they're not

55

worth a hair on your head." She put her head next to his. They hugged a moment longer. Then she said, "Look – blue nails."

Thomas Moon looked at his mother's paint-stained fingers and a watery laugh welled up. "Looks like blue skin – my mum's an alien," he joked, pretty weakly, he knew.

"I'm doing the kitchen next." Mrs Moon got out a paint chart. "Orange or yellow – I'll show you."

The paint chart swam in front of him as Thomas Moon searched it through tears. His mother's words glowed in his chest. *They're not worth a hair on your head.*

"That one – or that one." Mrs Moon pointed out an orange, then a yellow. "I can do it in an afternoon. With green paintwork – what do you think?"

"I think you'd better ask Dad."

Thomas kept his voice steady. *An astronaut never lets emotions interfere with transmissions to Mission Control. I'm not showing it hurts me. Over.* He watched the top of his mother's head as she pored over the paint chart and noticed with fascination that she had quite a few white hairs.

"Mum," he said after a moment, "why *am* I an only child?"

Mrs Moon looked up. "I didn't want you to be. It's just the way things turned out."

"I wish they hadn't."

"Me, too. I'd love you to have had a brother or a sister. But things aren't so bad, are they?"

"'Course not. Things are good."

Thomas tried to smile, feeling again that familiar sickly feeling that he ought to be grateful. Hadn't he always had the best of things? Both his parents' attention? Big presents at Christmas and birthdays? Treats no one in a big family had? More pocket money and space? No one to borrow his things? But somehow it didn't make up for it. Not by a million miles. Feeling permanently ungrateful made it worse. He'd swap it all, no question, for a brother or a sister like, but not like, himself.

Someone like, but not like, himself – an unimaginable brother or a sister. Sometimes he dreamed he came face to face with someone so like himself he *knew* it was his brother or his sister – and then, in dreams like these, he knew how much he wanted it to happen. It always amazed Thomas Moon how little people with brothers or sisters seemed to value them. He couldn't imagine it himself. It would be like looking into a mirror and seeing how you might have been – a different variation on yourself. Most of all, it meant *you weren't alone*.

If you were an only child, you felt like nobody else. Nobody knew how you felt. You had no one who *understood*. The tight little triangle you made with your parents grew tighter and tighter like a screw, and there wasn't anywhere to take it. Plus they made you feel one of a kind – why wouldn't they, your parents were proud of you, weren't they? Wanting you to be happy? But the weight of being happy was the weight of having everything on you.

Sometimes Thomas felt so big and so singular he couldn't walk down the street without feeling abashed. He couldn't join in at parties. He knew he was too self-conscious, but it didn't help at all. It wasn't that he thought he was better than anyone else, it was just that he didn't feel the *same*.

I'd love you to have had a brother or a sister. But things aren't so bad, are they?

His mother had had brothers and sisters. She didn't understand at all. The weight of being extraordinary pressed down on Thomas Moon with ten times the gravity of Saturn.

TRAINING

He did not try to learn what he was taught. As a matter of fact, he could not learn it. He could not, because his soul was full of more urgent claims...

– *Anna Karenina*, Tolstoy

Thomas woke up and knew he was inside a spacesuit. Sealed in with his thoughts. Distant from all other beings.

The suspension had come in quite handy. For one thing it meant he could train, uninterrupted by school, by other people, by any other distractions.

"Thomas! Breakfast!"

You're suspended, Quinlan had said. As from now.

"We'll see about that," Thomas's mother had flung back furiously, "at the Governors' meeting next week."

"Of course, your right of appeal—"

"Will be exercised, don't you worry."

"It's a matter of *principle*," Mr Quinlan had said, as the meeting had continued in his office.

"You're not overreacting, then," Mr Moon had cut in. "Throwing mint imperials around at *The Merchant of Venice* – not crime of the century, is it?"

"I'm afraid you miss the point, Mr Moon." Mr Quinlan had folded his hands and put on his regretful smile. "On any school visit, pupils represent the school. This was a complaint from a *member of the public*."

"I'm not listening to claptrap like this." Mr Moon rose angrily. "What Thomas did was thoughtless, but it doesn't rate suspension."

"I'm sorry you feel that way, Mr Moon."

"They didn't mean any harm," said Mrs Moon. "I think it was just high spirits."

"High spirits or not, Mrs Moon, I'm sure you'll appreciate the *seriousness*— "

"We're not excusing Thomas. It was a stupid thing to do. I don't know why he did it – he *likes* plays usually – he's in with a bad crowd, I think—"

"I'm afraid, Mrs Moon, that's what every parent says."

"I know he shouldn't have done it, but don't you think you could—"

"No matter how much I should like to overlook it – " Quinlan showed his teeth in a charmless smile to show how much he'd have *liked* to have overlooked it " – on this occasion I can't. I'm afraid the press have got hold of it. The school has been let down badly."

"How about Thomas?" his father put in. "Doesn't this let *him* down?"

"I'm sorry, Mr Moon?"

"His best friend's just moved away. He's a bit of a loner at the best of times – how's *this* going to make him feel?"

"You'd better ask him that," said Quinlan.

They all turned to look at Thomas.

Static was interfering with Thomas's reception. *Shame and remorse, come in, please. I'm sorry, do you read? Embarrassment, come in.* Sorry, nothing but resentment. He couldn't feel a thing. Thomas switched off his attention, and the white noise of space rushed in.

"Sorry," he mumbled, "what did you say?"

"Thomas – " His mother's jaw dropped. "– haven't you even been *listening*?"

"No." Thomas maintained a steely tone. Astronauts never made mistakes. They simply made re-calculations. "No," he said, "not specially."

The newspaper rang his mother the very next day. His mother was unrecognizable over the phone. Fierce, like a tiger or something. Thomas hardly knew her. His face burned as

61

he earwagged upstairs. It burned even more over the *Evening Herald*. It wasn't what he wanted, at all. It would look bad on any CV:

BOUNDARY ROAD PUPILS
SUSPENDED IN THEATRE DEBACLE

Brilliant. What was he – Mission Specialist in shooting himself in the foot? This wasn't about to impress any astronaut selection committee. Would they let someone in a *theatre debacle* control a remote manipulator arm or calculate orbital correction? They would, Thomas thought, because they'd never know. Not if he never told them. But he felt more sealed in than ever.

In the kitchen, his parents rowed fiercely about the situation, and Thomas stayed out of the way. His father had sat him down the previous night for the kind of Serious Talk that left Thomas's heart in his space-boots. Now that he was suspended from school, his father had said, he mustn't let things slide. The situation wouldn't last long. But while it did, the best thing to do was to draw up a timetable and stick to it. Study and exercise, that was the key. Thomas had his own timetable to stick to. But still he'd agreed to Dad's. Dad had gone off to World of Cladding next morning satisfied that they'd understood each other. Thomas was good at chats with Dad. He knew what he wanted to hear. Still, he ached to be understood. But only Mint could hear him.

Thomas's airless world that day included the Gun Room Gym. He'd promised to stay in and study. Instead, he worked off some rage. About five hundred calories' worth, in fact. Enough to stay in trim. Or make Payload Specialist, hopefully.

"Although Payload Specialists are not part of the Astronaut Candidate Program," the NASA Website pages had told Thomas, "they may be added to shuttle crews if activities that have unique requirements are involved."

What unique requirements, Thomas had wondered. He'd been thinking for some time that maybe he could be a Payload Specialist. Clearly it depended on what the payload was.

"Payload Specialists must have the appropriate education and training related to the payload or the equipment. All applicants must meet certain physical requirements and must pass NASA space physical examinations with varying standards depending on classification."

All applicants must meet certain physical requirements. The Gun Room Gym that day was particularly smelly and stuffy. Thomas Moon worked moodily round the equipment in no particular order, making his legs hurt first and then his arms, noting the muscle men in the weights section, trying out things he didn't usually touch at all, like the complicated

Pecs Press in the corner. *All applicants must meet certain physical requirements.* Fifteen Abdominal Crunches ... nineteen, twenty, twenty-one. *And must pass NASA space physical examinations...*

The guns on the walls of the Gun Room Gym looked down on Thomas Moon. They were real guns, all right. That was the whole point. The reason it was called the Gun Room Gym was that before it had become a gym, it had been a gun room. Thomas Moon knew next to nothing about guns, but as he worked out beneath them he thought about what guns could do. The posters beneath them jumped out and told him stuff –

- HEARTBEAT HEALTH
- HOW TO DO EXERCISES WITHOUT ANY WEIGHTS
- STEP CHALLENGE
- MARATHON CHALLENGE
- ADVENTURE SPORTS FOR YOU
- WHITE WATER CANOEING – sign up with Greg at the desk

– while he rowed himself half to *death*. MTV played on all screens. Then a loud American programme came on, a bit like *Blind Date* on fast-forward at some cheesy American summer camp where everyone had tans and jumped in swimming pools screaming. Thomas wondered what it was all about. Then he got up and showered. Rowing one kilo-metre in 4.06 seconds was enough physical requirements for *anyone*.

He walked moodily home past the hardware store, where he went in and asked for the largest hook they had in stock. He was pleased with it when he'd bought it. It felt like serious equipment. Well-tooled and heavy-duty.

"Thomas," said Thomas's mother when he got in, "I've written a letter for the Governors' meeting, and so has Philip's mother – would you like to see what we've written?"

"Not really," Thomas said, sourly.

"It might make all the difference."

Thomas shrugged. "Once a spacecraft's holed, you're going to lose air-pressure, aren't you?"

"What are you talking about?"

"Me and Tedious and Barry. Quinlan's go-ing to blow us out, no matter what you say."

"Not necessarily." Mrs Moon looked at Thomas. She was going to say something else, but then she said, "Are you all right?"

"Not really," Thomas repeated. "I'm going up to my room."

Downloading the latest mail, Thomas found something new from Mint:

```
Return-Path: <Mint@Mint.ogre.co.uk
From: Mint<Mint@Mint.ogre.co.uk
To: Thomas.Moon@gremlin.net
```

Date: Fri 31 May 16:52:05 GMTOBST
Subject: Eat Your Heart Out
Moonie,
Eat your heart out when you know
I've got tickets for Gladiators. I
got them through my cousin because
my cousin's best friend's
boyfriend's going in for it, and
he's like, really fit? Birmingham
Arena on the 24th. My cousins are
doing banners and stuff. Should be
cool or what.
School's pretty putrid. They don't
even have a canteen, you just sit
out and eat on the grass, plus
when they let the Year Eleven ani-
mals out I usually get my bag
kicked in or I get my dinner
nicked.
Mum and Dad really like it up
here, but I wish we never came. My
room's OK, not brilliant. Probably
after Gladiators it might be
better.
That spaceman stuff's weird. How
did you get selected for Astronaut
Status? Is it a joke, or what? I
don't get who's sending you messages.
Later,
Ludlow Shropshire

Thomas felt worse than ever reading Mint. Mint was in a different universe already. Mint didn't know that he, Thomas Moon, had been suspended. He didn't know about *The Merchant of Venice*. He didn't know anything at all. Thomas reread his message. It seemed about a million years since he'd even set eyes on Mint. Wait a minute – what was that? Right at the bottom of the screen – underneath Ludlow Shropshire?

Thomas paged down with a jumping heart. There – a *Text File Attached tag!* A secret message bundled under something else! Just like the last two times! Rapidly accessing TXT lists, Thomas scanned unopened entries. There it was, Text_3.TXT. A brand-new message to – or from – Mister Spaceman.

Sly, Thomas thought. An email from Mint. *And attached to it, an SPM29:*

```
Return-Path: <SPM29@starlight.ac.uk
From: SPM29<SPM29@starlight.ac.uk
To: Thomas.Moon@gremlin.net
Date: Fri 31 May 16:52:05 GMTOBST
Subject: Rigorous Training Directive
Content-Type: text/plain
Content-Description: Text_3
Content-Disposition: attachment
filename="Text_3.TXT"
Attachment Converted:
C:\COMMS\PANDORA\Text_15.TXT
```

```
RIGOROUS TRAINING DIRECTIVE
STIPULATED HOURS IN THE SIMULATOR
OVER FINAL FIVE WEEKS = THIRTY
HOURS.
WEIGHTLESS ENVIRONMENT TRAINING
FACILITY (WETF) TEN HOURS PER
WEEK.
IMPORTANT YOU LOG TRAINING HOURS.
OVER.
MISSION CONTROL
```

Thomas gobbled the directive whole. Could it really mean what it was telling him? Weightless Environment Training Facility – that meant the swimming pool – but ten hours per *week*? For the final five weeks? Thirty hours' SMS (Shuttle Mission Simulator). Ten hours, WETF. That would take some doing. He'd have to step up his hours in the pool. Do way more Golding's Hotel, plus maybe the Belvedere Hotel, as well – maybe overnight – that would clock up almost half his MSH, or Mandated Simulator Hours.

Now at least he had something to aim at. Something to tell him what to do. Was this stuff real? What was he, kidding himself? Right now he was mentally exhausted, the way he'd probably feel after three hours' welding in space.

That night, Mrs Carrier sent him some French and a note. The note said:

Dear Thomas,

The quality of mercy seems a bit strained at the moment, but don't worry too much and keep up your French. I know we will see you back in school before too long –

Best wishes,

Louise Carrier

Best wishes, Louise Carrier. I read you. Over and out. Thomas turned the French books in his hands, then read some *Famille Delarge*, but it didn't help much at all. Poor Mister Spaceman. No one could reach him now, not even people who cared. In some way he'd lifted off already.

Later Mister Spaceman lay in bed practising correction of directional thrusters by the stars. In space, he would sleep standing up, hooked to a wall in his sleeping bag. With no gravity to keep him in it, his sleeping bag would be zipped all the way up, to prevent him floating out. It didn't matter to him which way up he slept. There *was* no "up" in space. The only fixed points were the stars.

It was important to know the stars, in case navigational equipment packed up. Thomas Moon ran over them in his mind. The stars would look different in space. What he needed was an orbital map. Meanwhile, he could practise, couldn't he? Pick out the Pole Star, Rigel, Sirius, Canopus, Andromeda? Andromeda was actually a *galaxy*. Hubble had discovered it, and had had a space telescope named after him when he was dead. Before Hubble realized Andromeda was a galaxy in 1926, no one knew about other galaxies at all. They thought our galaxy was the only one. Big and special and *singular*.

Thomas sighed and turned out the light. No one could get away from themselves, least of all him. He *was* his own universe. And nothing could ever change it, or help him escape.

THE SIMULATOR

Return-Path: <Thomas.Moon@gremlin.net
From: TCM24<Thomas.Moon@gremlin.net
To: Mint@Mint.ogre.co.uk
Date: Tue 7 Jun 22:03:57 GMTOBST
Subject: Mission Update
Yo Ludlow, or Mint if you're there —
being suspended's OK, did I tell
you I got suspended? It means I can
train all day and no one bugs me.
This morning I did Golding's Hotel.
The lifts make wicked simulators.
I jam 'em between two floors, and
see how long I can handle it? It's
amazing how quickly you forget
where you are. Also you lose track
of time. It was pretty hairy today
but I lasted out. I have to do
stipulated SMS — that's Shuttle
Mission Simulator — hours on my

own. I might be alone in space.
Mum's gone and painted the kitchen
yellow. She painted the spice rack
onto the wall, also a fly or two.
What next, I said, a red bathroom?
She laughed, but you can't relax.
She doesn't tell you what she's
going to do, she just does it. I
could come home and she's painted
over my bedroom. I'd move out if
she painted over my bedroom. She
painted Dad's Dinky cars once. She
thought they looked scratched, but
Dad went ape. They're antiques, he
goes. I've had them for years, now
you've ruined them. Someday she'll
paint over something really important. Good thing she's stuck in
the shop all week. She does things
in too much hurry.
Still waiting for my next directive from Mission Control. Waiting's important. I can do that.
Governors' meeting next week.
Tedious and Neil and Barry all got
their parents to write, plus Mum
and Dad wrote too. They're going
to appeal, but I wish they
wouldn't. Being suspended is cool.
See the game last night?
Over and out.

The simulator had proved pretty interesting – if you *liked* featureless silver boxes – over the course of the one-and-a-half-hour-long stint Thomas had spent in it that morning, something he hadn't, in fact, ever attempted before. Of course, he'd jammed the lift before. But this time he'd meant to stay in it.

It was easy to jam the service lifts at Golding's Hotel. Pressing all the buttons at once put them out of synch, so they stopped between floors every time. Usually they sorted themselves out if you waited and punched a few buttons. But this time, Thomas didn't want them to. He'd been counting on some serious SMS hours.

Thomas had discovered the secret stairway to the service lifts at Golding's Hotel by accident. The service lifts at Golding's Hotel had a hi-tech look and an unfussy way of operating that made Thomas think of spacecraft. As work-a-day elevators for the staff, they had none of the frills, gilt or mirrors of the plush-looking lifts in the lobby. They were simply silver boxes with a phone. They rushed up and down all day filled with chambermaids or waiters or head housekeepers or stewards with trolleys carrying extravagant dinners covered in gleaming silver domes that the waiter whipped off to show you a lobster looking up at you from a bed of lettuce. Thomas Moon had never stayed in a hotel in his life, so he didn't know too much about them. That was the reason he'd discovered the secret stairway at Golding's Hotel in the first place.

The first time he'd ever set foot in Golding's Hotel, Thomas had been required to. Mr Dart had told Thomas's class to find out all they could about local hotels for their Leisure and Tourism projects, due in at the end of the term. Thomas had nerved himself to go in one day on his way home from school to pick up a Golding's brochure. The gilt and glass revolving doors had thrown him into a lobby murmurous with the hushed tones of staff and guests, filled with hard, clean surfaces that shone or gleamed or offered you flowers or a chance to sit down with the papers. On an occasional table by the reception desk Thomas noticed a box chocked with notepaper and leaflets: *Golding's for Four-star Service – Conferences * Fitness Weekends * Spa * Multigym * Heated Pool * Golding's – Your Lifestyle Choice for Premier Relaxation*. Thomas looked around. They were glossy-looking leaflets. Was it all right just to take one? Finally he helped himself, half-waiting for someone to stop him. He felt clumsy and out of place in this smooth, tinkling world of the lobby, and he wasn't the only one. The glittering lobby had impressed him, but on his way back past the reception desk he'd heard a woman complain:

"I don't *like* lifts. I like a hotel with *stairs*."

"Yes – we don't have stairs, I'm afraid."

"I can see that," the woman huffed.

"Sorry about that." The receptionist smiled. "I can put you on the ground floor."

"If you could," the woman grumped. "I feel closed in in lifts."

Thomas had nosed around, and no one had even noticed. He'd even used the toilets in the lobby, profoundly amazed by the scents and sounds and mirrors, by the plush-feeling fall of his own two feet on carpets thick as duvets. On his way out past the toilets, he noticed some discreet double doors. FIRE EXIT ONLY they said. Thomas Moon nosed through them and found himself looking up a windy and unglamorous concrete stairway. They *do* have stairs, he thought. Why did they say they hadn't? Thomas slipped in and went up them. Before he knew it, he'd raced up a whole lot more, just to see where they led to. They didn't seem to lead anywhere, except higher and higher into the building. 1a–1b. Each half-floor stage had a letter. 2a–2b, 3a–3b – Collection Point Here. Collection for what? Thomas wondered.

The glamour and swish of the lobby left behind him, Thomas had bounded with electric ease from floor to floor to floor. Occasional fire extinguishers marked each third floor stage, but he met no one and saw no one, and saw no reason to stop. The fourth floor had smelled of laundry, the second of kitchens. A sign on the third had said: WAVES FITNESS SUITE – PLEASE DRESS SUITABLY BETWEEN WAVES AND YOUR ROOM. THANK YOU.

Thomas climbed higher and higher. He looked down the giddy stairwell. A man in white crossed a floor far beneath him with a tray. The smash and crash of the second-floor kitchens wafted up. This was a side of Golding's no one was supposed to see. It was thrilling, somehow, to spy on it. The inner workings of the great hotel were going on all around him – and no one dreamed he was there! The concrete staircase was part of the feeling, thought Thomas. Windy, rough-edged and smelly, spotted with grease and grime and not at all like the glossy foyer, it was a secret passage – his secret way in – to the heart of Golding's Hotel.

Through the double doors on floor seven, he came upon his first service lift. A plain metal box with a phone, it whisked Thomas down to GROUND so fast he felt a draught on his head. He'd even had a moment of weightlessness when it had lurched on, starting and stopping.

What a rush, Thomas had thought. *Wicked simulator*. He'd been back a few times since then. He knew that the silver lifts plunged up and down all day and most of the night, sometimes clinking with crockery, sometimes stiff with under-chefs, because he'd watched them. They wouldn't, of course, be real Shuttle Mission Simulator hours he would be spending inside them. But they were as close as he was going to get. The service lifts at Golding's Hotel *simulated* the feeling of being cut off in a silver box pretty well, especially when you imagined 'em turning in space with the earth revolving grandly beneath them. Except there *was* no beneath or above, only the numberless stars. If you thought about it, it was a real practice, in any case. Wouldn't he be in a box, on a *planet* that was turning in space? There was no way he wasn't an astronaut. Thomas, and everyone else.

That morning Thomas Moon had slipped into service lift B4 at Golding's Hotel at about eleven o'clock and jammed it pretty thoroughly. The staff would have to use service lifts B5 and B6. No one would bother too much. The lifts were hardly ever all working at once.

He sat down and spread out his kit. Skipping-rope for exercise. Coke for dehydration. Tubed food for – food. Cyberpet for company. So here he was, stuck in a spacecraft. How would he feel in orbit, twelve miles above the earth? He'd have things to do, of course. Instruments to check. But this would be his world. Except for the stars outside, a very small world indeed. But still it would be a *new* world. The thought of it made him tingle.

The whine and suck of passing lift B6 interrupted Thomas's dream. With no trouble at all he changed the sound it made into the straining of the robot arm outside the spacecraft as it blindly made adjustments to the solar panel mountings. The minutes passed really slowly. Then they passed really fast. He'd made it a rule to have no watch. An astronaut's time would be synchronized with Mission Control, in any case. The different regional time zones on earth would be meaningless in orbit.

Thomas Moon felt his thoughts drift away into space. He could do this, he knew it, if only he could once get the chance. *He* could grow plants from seeds in space and sleep upright and eat out of tubes and not get upset with other people in a very confined space and put up with the shunt and drag of fantastic acceleration on ditching first-stage boosters. If he could only *try*. The walls of the silver lift could have been any walls, in any spacecraft, anywhere. Outside lay the cold kiss of space, that would crush him without his EVA suit without a second's pause. But Thomas Moon wasn't afraid. Something in him wanted the edge – the very edge of space, the very edge of *himself*.

Soon he forgot where he was, who he was, the passage of time, the—

Ber-ber – ber-ber – ber-ber – ber-ber –

Thomas jumped up – what? Where? Something was ringing and ringing – the phone – *the phone on the wall of the lift.*

With an effort, Thomas Moon remembered where he was.

Ber-ber – ber-ber – ber-ber –

It wasn't going to stop.

Ber-ber – ber-ber – ber-ber –

At last he picked up the phone.

"Service lift B4?" the phone enquired. "Hello? Anyone there?"

Uh-oh. *Response imperative.* This had never happened before.

"Mission Control, come in, please." Thomas cleared his throat. "Space Station Moon. Over."

"This is Mission Control," the voice joked cheerfully. "Maintenance Engineer – have you been stuck long?"

Have you been stuck long? Thomas had no idea. But still he would have to say something. Transmissions from space were usually terse and filled with relevant data. He loved the way astronauts spoke, the cool way they understated things. Here he was stuck in a lift. What would an *astronaut* say?

"Simulation commenced eleven hundred hours," he tried, cautiously. "We are A-OK."

"You might be A-OK now, but you won't be in three hours' time," the cheerful voice advised him. "Can you look at your control panel for me?"

"We copy your request. Over."

"Is your panel showing a red light?" the cheerful voice went on. "Is it floor three or floor four?"

Thomas considered the lift control panel. A light – more orange than red – blinked alongside the numbered floor buttons.

"All systems stasis, we have a code orange here," Thomas announced, as laconically as he could.

"Floor three or floor four?"

"Confirm three. Over."

"Right, I can see your problem." Thomas could practically hear the engineer checking his equipment, pushing back his hat, taking his time to think it over. "Can you see there's a black button – all on its own – at the bottom left of your panel?"

Thomas kept cool and collected. He knew he could handle an emergency in space. This was the way to handle it.

"We copy your black button, bottom of panel. Over."

"Can you push it for me?"

Thomas pressed the black button. The lift

jolted, hiccuped, stopped.

"Now can you press floor four?"

"Affirmative. Pressing floor four."

Thomas pressed the button numbered four. The lift shuddered, started, stopped, started again, gained speed, rushed up its shaft, and threw him out on floor four, where he burst through some steaming laundry rooms and out through the fire-exit doors and down the echoing, stained concrete stairway and out of Golding's by the back way before the faceless but cheerful maintenance engineer could remonstrate with him or catch him.

Still going over events in his mind, Thomas went home the long way round, by the dockyard, on an errand he'd been meaning to do for some time. Afterwards he felt better. When he finally got in he clumped upstairs to his room and did some thinking. He rearranged some data files on computer. Then he lay on the floor and reread astronaut Joe Allen's description of suiting up for EVA. *Your shipmates bundle you up... They put the helmet over your head, snap it into place at the neck ring, and from that moment on you float in the suit... Everything must be checked, especially the seals... Everything goes on in order...*

What did being sealed in a spacesuit *feel* like, Thomas wondered. After a moment he got up and turned out his bedroom drawers. He got out all the shorts and T-shirts he could find and laid them out on the floor. Then he put them on, in the order he'd laid them out in. Then he put on all three of his track suits, one on top of another. Then he went into his parents' bedroom and put on three of his father's, saving the largest till last. When at last he turned to look at himself in the mirror, he found he could hardly walk.

A figure in a fat-suit stared back at him. So he didn't look like Tom Hanks in *Apollo 13*, what was important here was *feel*. Weight for weight, he wouldn't have believed how restricting the equivalent of a full EVA suit could be. Now he was glad he'd tried it. And there was still the weight of his Life Support, plus a Manned Manoeuvring Unit.

Cheered by the way it was all falling into place, Thomas scoured the house for a bulky Unit Simulator. In the end, he weighted his rucksack to mimic an MMU. A smaller rucksack on his front represented his Portable Life Support System. Satisfied that he'd got as close to EVA bulk and weight as he was going to, Thomas headed for the garage.

Some time later, the Moons' up-and-over garage door rose slowly over a spaceman. Slowly the spaceman emerged into the light of a sunny afternoon. The sunlight flashed off his helmet – a full-face motorcycle helmet. Bending with all the grace of a statue brought to life, he closed the garage door with a motorcycle-gloved hand. Slowly he turned and made the first of many ponderous steps down the road in motorcycle boots too large for him, perfecting his walk as he went.

The walk was really important. Thomas Moon had seen enough spacemen bounding around on the moon to believe he knew how they moved. It wasn't so easy in the equivalent of a full EVA suit affected by gravity. But with an effort he could manage a rolling walk, even if he'd die of heat-exhaustion before he reached the end of the road. A proper multi-layered EVA suit would have liquid-cooled garments beneath it, of course, instead of a million T-shirts. Thomas rolled away down the road, giving himself the wedgie of all time as he went, as his shorts bunched under his track suits and he puffed and blew inside his father's motorcycle helmet, which restricted his vision extremely – and as he rolled, he thought. He could go into school, why not? Technically not barred from school premises so long as he wasn't in uniform, that honour having been removed from him for throwing mint imperials, no one could actually stop him.

By the time he reached the playing fields, Thomas was in a world of his own. Inside his simulated suit, heat had built to epic propor-tions. He could practically power a power station, or heat a minor suburb with the incredible head of steam he'd raised by walking. And all he could do was walk. Puff, roll, blow. Puff, roll, blow. Try to see where you're going. He couldn't even adjust his visor, so hard was it to lift his arm. He guessed it felt like 3 Gs pressure – the pressure you felt on lift-off, when gravity pressed you so hard in your seat, you felt you weighed three times as much.

Rolling over the hockey pitch in exaggerated slow-motion, Thomas Moon was aware that he'd cause a stir. He could hear the chairs in classrooms 1 to 4 E scraping and falling over as Years Seven to Ten in Main Block noticed the spaceman on the field. He wished he could notice *himself*. It was what he'd always imagined, always dreamed about, up there behind those third-floor windows, during those mind-numbingly dull afternoons when the clock-hands ticked but never moved. Today he was his own dream – a spaceman appearing out of nowhere. He'd have died to have been up there in classroom 3B and seen himself.

"Please, Mr Benchley, there's a spaceman out on the field."

"Pull yourself together, Moon."

"Look, sir! See for yourself!"

"My God, Moon, you're right!"

Thomas Moon grinned inside his helmet. It was worth the effort to come into school to light up everyone's lives. They had to have seen him by now. Thomas Moon put on a spurt. Bounding along parallel with the building in his best imitation of the last spacewalk a spaceman might manage before dropping dead of heatstroke, he tried giving Main Block a wave, dimly glimpsing as he passed them windows sticky with faces and hands, some hands waving, some not.

He moonwalked on towards the cricket pitch, hearing his breath in his helmet, feeling the beating of his heart, reporting to base as he went. *The surface seems rigid but slippery, over. We have some white lines at right angles to one another ... and a net-like structure... I'm going over to investigate...* Dimly aware that Mr Sumner, the caretaker, had spotted him, Thomas felt panic welling up. *This could be hostile terrain, do you read?* Oh, well – suspended, wasn't he? He might as well be suspended in something. He'd be up to his neck in it anyway if Mr Quinlan had seen him.

Mr Sumner approached him warily with a rake. Thomas wondered what he'd say. In the end, he said, "Stop right there."

Thomas stopped. Stopping was easy.

Mr Sumner's mouth worked. "Have you got an identity card?" he asked, absurdly.

"Do I *look* like I've got an identity card?" Thomas said inside his helmet, but it came out, "Bloo-bli-*blook*-I-blot-I-blenni-bard?"

"What?" Mr Sumner screwed up his eyes. He had to ask *everyone on school premises*, regardless of how strange they looked – *especially* if they looked strange – if they had an identity card. Identity cards were Mr Quinlan's latest fixation. Everyone had to have one on school premises, even Mr Sumner, in case he forgot who he was, even Mr Quinlan himself, in case he wouldn't let himself in.

"You'd better come with me." Mr Sumner's eyes popped. Thomas realized he was frightened. "I can't tell who you are, in all that get-up."

Thomas felt annoyed. "I don't have to," he told the inside of his helmet. "I'm not doing anything wrong."

"I can't hear a word you're saying." Mr Sumner advanced his rake. "Think you're funny, do you?"

Suddenly Thomas crumpled – it wasn't hard. He felt as though he was suffocating. He could hardly see Mr Sumner, let alone hear him. He hardly felt the ground as he fell – he hardly fell at all. He simply collapsed in his suit. Through his steamed-up visor he could just see Mr Sumner's shoes and the bottoms of his gardening trousers.

Mr Sumner was disconcerted. He walked all round the spaceman one way, then the other. Then he poked him with the end of his rake.

"Wakey, wakey – time to get up."

Thomas Moon lay perfectly still. It was so good not to have to walk.

"Come on – let's be 'aving you."

Finally Mr Sumner bent down and peered anxiously into Thomas's helmet – closer, closer – suddenly Thomas raised his Michelin-Man arm and laid it on Mr Sumner's neck.

Mr Sumner jumped a mile. He darted back for his rake, then darted away again.

"You don't get me that way," he said. "I'm calling the p'lice now you did that," he said, "so *don't you go away.*"

He didn't feel much like going away. He felt dizzy and hot and cross. With an enormous effort, Thomas Moon got up.

"Stay back," warned Mr Sumner. "I don't want any tricks."

Thomas Moon tore off his helmet and drank in fresh air. "It's only me, Mr Sumner."

"Me who?"

"Thomas Moon from 9G."

"You can take that smile off your face. What do you think you look like?"

"Like a spaceman," Thomas said. "Except I had to use track suits."

"You look like a bleddy bank robber."

"Sorry if I scared you."

Thomas Moon. In track suits. And a motor-cycle helmet. Mr Sumner turned, uneasily aware that he'd made a fool of himself in front of everyone in Main Block. Just as he'd feared, the whole weight of Years Eight and Nine had their faces pressed to the windows. The windows would probably fall out, and then he'd have to replace them. Mr Sumner recovered himself. "We'll see what Mr Quinlan has to say. Then you won't find it so funny."

"I'm not allowed in school," said Thomas sweetly.

"Never mind all that. Just you follow me."

"I can't," said Thomas sweetly. "I'm suspended, remember? You can't make me go *any*where."

And he raised his arms to Main Block in a salute – *yeah!* – and most of Main Block waved back – *way to go, Spaceman!*

Mr Sumner looked lost for a moment. "Get off out of it, then," he growled.

"We copy your Get Off Out of It." Thomas Moon put on his helmet. "Complying now, over and out."

And he turned and rolled off over the field, puffing and blowing as he went. Mr Sumner watched him go. Behind Mr Sumner in Main Block, beneath the crowded floors that stared down at him, a red-faced fish gaped in Quinlan's ground-floor office. The red-faced fish was Mr Quinlan. Spotting a spaceman for the first time. Out on the school playing fields. In the amazing shape of *Thomas Moon*.

Mr Quinlan recovered himself. He opened his office window and applied his face to the gap.

"Mr Sumner! Mr Sumner! Mr Sumner!"

Mr Sumner watched the spaceman cross the hockey field, then the football pitch beyond. He watched him grow smaller and smaller with his funny, rolling walk, and the further away he went, the more convincing he looked. Talk about close encounters. Mr Sumner felt quite peculiar. When the spaceman had disappeared altogether, Mr Sumner turned away and remembered where he was and what he was supposed to be doing and what a perfect prat he'd made of himself, and how the school had seen it. That boy Moon had a screw loose, anyone could see. Hadn't Moon been in Mr Quinlan's office when he'd strimmed through that muck the other day? Bit unfortunate, that. Unfortunate Moon had seen him.

"Mr Sumner! Can you hear me! Is that Thomas Moon?"

Waving vaguely at Mr Quinlan, Mr Sumner made for the flower-beds. They wouldn't take long to weed and rake out. Not in this summer sunshine.

MISTER SPACEMAN

The new blue carpet felt alien, like the surface of some strange new planet. The No Shoes rule didn't help.

Thomas Moon traversed the living-room in his stockinged feet.

We have surface resistance...

He watched a bit of telly. Then he emailed Mint.

```
Return-Path: <Thomas.Moon@gremlin.net
From: TCM24<Thomas.Moon@gremlin.net
To: Mint@Mint.ogre.co.uk
Date: Fri 10 Jun 17:31:28 GMTOBST
Subject: T Minus Four Weeks and
Counting
Dear Ludlow Shropshire,
I had a row with Dad the other
night. I tried to tell him, you
know? I really tried to tell him,
```

I'm really Mister Spaceman. I'm
going to do it, I said. You don't
think I can, but I will. I don't
think he believed me. It'll all
blow over, he goes. All this
going-into-space stuff. You'll grow
out of it, in time. It might grow
out of me, I said, I won't grow
out of it. What's wrong with being
an astronaut? What's wrong with
having ambitions? It's all very
well, Dad goes, but you're not
even in school. So? I said, everyone has to start somewhere. Yes,
Dad goes, but you, you're going
backwards.

Anyway, you don't want to know.
What I did do the other day is, I
got her name and address off Mrs
Easterhouse, and I went round to
see the woman who complained in
The Murderer of Vengeance, sorry,
The Merchant of Venice, to let her
know I was sorry? Turns out her
name's Mrs Innes and she's only
partially sighted. She only goes
to the theatre to hear the
speeches. No wonder we teed her
off. You were really annoying, she
said. I know we were, I said. I'm
really sorry, I said. I don't

blame you for complaining. I'd
complain if I were you. Get into
much trouble? she said. Loads, I
said. The most. And then I told
her. She thought it was really
stupid we got suspended. She
thought we'd just get told off.
I'm hacked off I missed the play,
I said. That was the worst thing
about it.
Then we got talking. I'm on my own
quite a lot, she said. Funny, I
said, so am I. Don't you have any
brothers or sisters? she goes.
You're joking, I said, brothers
and sisters? Brothers and sisters
are a pain. I stayed and talked
for ages. In the end I felt really
bad. Couldn't you go again, I
said. The play's still on, I said.
I'll buy your ticket this time.
You better go soon, I said. Old
Antonio'll be sick of having his
heart almost cut out every night.
Know what she said? She said, I
don't want to see that play again.
I'd think of you sitting out and
missing it. Then she goes: Would
you like me to write to your
school? A letter from me might do
the trick. It might make things

92

better, you know. That's not why I
came, I said. I know, she said,
but I want to. It's what I want to
do. But I don't write very good
letters. It's my eyesight, you
see. Then she goes: Can you clean
my windows? So — guess what — I
did.
So while I'm cleaning her windows
I get this idea. Why not synthe-
size a spacesuit, so at least I
know how it feels? So when I get
home I look up how much an EVA
suit weighs, then I pull on all
these track suits and stuff until
I weigh about right. By the time
I've got these layers and layers
of clothes on, it looks like a
fat-suit or something. But at
least I'm getting the feel of a
spacesuit, you know? I'm using my
initiative here? So I'm putting on
Dad's old crash helmet when I
start thinking, right, Why not go
into school?
So I go into school with this crap
on and Dad's full-face helmet on
my head and I do this spacewalk
thing on the field in front of
Main Block, third lesson? It
totally freaks old Sumner out, he

almost drops dead when I jump him.
Duncan Robards wet himself, I wish
you could have seen it.
But that's not what it's about.
What it's about is being prepared,
right, being space-fit when the
time comes. I know the clock's
ticking down. T minus four weeks
and counting.
T minus seven minutes — six
minutes — five — four —
Your favourite astronaut and mine
— three — two — one
WE HAVE IGNITION!
T.C. Moon

Let Mint find his way through that one.
It was long enough to send him to sleep.
He kissed the Gremlin goodbye, and the
Gremlin winked away. Still being good, are
we? Thomas Moon shut down.

He rummaged in his schoolbag. At last, at
the bottom, he found it; the hook he'd bought
at the hardware store – when? The other day?
It was a big brass hook. Sturdy. Strong. Space-
fit. Thomas Moon considered it. Then he went
to the garage and found his father's masonry
drill. A couple more trips to the garage, and he
had just about everything else he needed for
the job he had in mind. But first he'd need a
snack. First he thought he'd have cereal. Then

he thought of a space snack. Something a spaceman might have. In the end he settled for tomato purée and cream cheese, just because they were in tubes.

Some time later, he heard the car pull in. He heard his parents opening the front door, their whispered consultation in the hall. He heard the kettle go on. Then he heard his mother slowly climbing the stairs. They'd been to the Governors' meeting, he knew. That was why he felt sick.

Thomas Moon gunned the masonry drill into the hole he'd made in the wall.

Bub-bub-bub-rurrgull-bub.

A bit more. Not quite deep enough.

Rurr-rurr-bub. Rurr-bub.

Better. Not bad, in fact. He steeled himself to go on with the job. They couldn't hurt a spaceman already in space. He didn't care *what* had gone down.

"What on earth are you doing?"

Thomas's mother appeared round his bedroom door in the best suit he didn't like much. Her lipstick had worn off already. He wished she wouldn't wear red. He took his thumb off the drill trigger and examined the hole he'd made. He tried the hook inside it. Still not quite deep enough.

"Thomas – what are you doing?"

"Putting in a hook. What does it look like I'm doing?"

His mother regarded it doubtfully. "It's a big hook – what for?"

"To hang things on, perhaps?"

Thomas finished drilling the hole. *Fee-wee*, whined the masonry drill. *Fnee-wee-nee-fnee – rurr-bub-bub-bub*.

"You've been a long time," he said coldly.

"We stopped off to have a quick drink."

"Well?" Thomas said, "what happened?" *Can I get some guidance, here? Mission Control, come in, please.*

Thomas's mother frowned. "What I don't like about Mr Quinlan is, Mr Quinlan's so rude – "

"Tell me about it," Thomas said. "Plus he's mad, as well."

"He told us life was like a bicycle. I haven't a clue what he meant."

"Join the club." Thomas thumped in a Rawlplug. "So when do I go back to school?"

Thomas's mother blinked. "The thing is, it got quite nasty. Mrs Carrier was there – "

"Mrs *Carrier* was there?"

"Witness for the defence."

"And?"

"Well," – Mrs Moon looked vague – "well, when Mr Quinlan said life was like a bicycle, you'd had a bad fall, the lot of you, and you wouldn't be re-mounting it until the autumn term at least – "

"We're suspended till *September*?"

" – to give you time to mend the punctures, Mrs Carrier stood up and set them straight – the Governors, you know, Pritchard and Redneck and Pringle – and your dad and I practically cheered. Philip Tettios's father got up and shook her by the hand. You should've heard what she said."

Thomas tried the hook again. "Oh?" he said, and his heart beat fast. "So what *did* she say?"

"She was wonderful." Mrs Moon flushed. "Hasn't this gone far enough, she said. Wouldn't the boys concerned respect the system much more if you simply quashed this now? Wouldn't a little – temperance, I think she said – *temperance* now do more for the school's reputation than suspending these boys over something that should have been, and was, dealt with on the spot?"

"Then what?" Thomas asked. His heart beat faster still.

"Then she said, I can't speak for Neil or Philip or Barry, but I know Thomas Moon and I know how much it must have meant to him, to've had to miss the play."

Thomas's heart felt ready to burst. *He hadn't told her anything at all.* How had she known how he felt? Mrs Carrier was out on a limb – total EVA.

" 'He's a good student when he applies himself,' she said. 'I know he's inclined to dream,

97

but there's real gold underneath.'"

"What did Mr Quinlan say?" Thomas held his breath.

"That's when it got quite nasty. Mr Quinlan told Mrs Carrier to sit down, thank you, that wasn't the point. Then Mrs Carrier said, 'Excuse me, Mr Quinlan, but it's very *much* the point.' Then she asked him how much he knew about you all – turns out he didn't even know which *year* you were in, let alone what you were doing for English or anything else. Mrs Carrier said following form was no substitute for a real interest in students' welfare. Mr Pringle, he's one of the Governors, asked Mrs Carrier to repeat that, so then Mrs Carrier, she colours up and says..."

Thomas screwed in his hook. He could hardly see or hear what his mother was saying, so blurred were his eyes and ears. All the same, he heard the phone.

"Better get it," he mumbled somehow. "Might be important, for me."

It was important, and it was for him – the voice, of all others, he wanted, yet dreaded, to hear.

"*Bonjour*, Thomas?"

"Mrs Carrier?"

"Thomas, I'm sorry – have you heard?" Her voice sounded heavy and defeated. "Of course you'll have heard by now. I wanted you to know I did my best. Suspension till September

– it's ridiculous, of course. We tried to tell them why, but they didn't want to hear."

"Don't worry," said Thomas, struck by her voice. "I'll survive, I expect."

"Thomas, I'm sorry, I tried…"

"I know you did. Mum told me."

"It didn't make any difference. Nothing must interfere, you see, with the *reputation of the school*."

"It doesn't matter," Thomas said. "Thanks for trying, though."

"I won't be seeing you in September, now. So I hope it all works out."

"What d'you mean?" Thomas said, suddenly afraid. "Why won't I see you in September?"

"I resigned at the meeting, Thomas. I won't be back next term."

"You *resigned*?" Thomas said. "Over *me*?"

"Over a principle, I'm afraid."

Three seconds passed, then five. *Please take it back, Mrs Carrier. I can't do school without you. Come in, please, sense and reason. Reality check, start now.*

"Thomas? Are you there?"

Come in, Space Station Moon. Space Station Moon, do you read?

"Thomas? Hello? Hello?"

The white noise of space filled Thomas Moon's ears with the sound of immense isolation, isolation so dense and so far from an orbit around anyone else, it seemed like the last goodbye from the outermost moon of Pluto. Cut off so completely and utterly from any explanation of the way he felt that he couldn't even say goodbye, Thomas Moon dropped the phone and bolted out of the house. *Over and out, Mrs Carrier. We have no closure on this.*

"Thomas! Where are you going?"

Mrs Moon reached the open front door in time to see Thomas disappearing around the corner of the street. Thoughtfully she rescued the phone.

"Hello? I'm sorry, he's gone. Thank you for all you – one of those things, I'm afraid. I'm sure he will. Thank you. Goodbye."

Feeling anxious and slightly befuddled, Mrs Moon rejoined Thomas's dad.

"That was Mrs Carrier," she said. "She wondered where he'd got to. Thomas ran off down the road."

Thomas's father grunted. "Give him a chance to think."

"He'll be upset she's resigned."

"He'll get over it," Thomas's dad said. "Any more of that coffee?"

Mrs Moon refilled his cup.

"I don't like it," she said. "He's screwing a hook in the wall."

"What d'you mean – a hook?"

"To hang something on – I don't know. It's

a great big hook, I don't know what for. He borrowed your masonry drill."

"He did, did he?" Thomas's father said, darkly.

"I'm worried, Colin. He's not like himself, at all – hasn't been, for a while."

"He didn't ask me if he could borrow it."

"I don't know what's got into him."

"Borrowing tools without asking. It's not like him not to ask."

"That's what I'm *saying*. Can't you see? What's the matter with him lately?"

"That's a good drill, that is," Thomas's father said thoughtfully. "He'd better not have blunted the bits."

Mrs Innes's house loomed like a cliff at the border of unknown territory, where the piles of Gervis Mansions met the steely-looking walls of the dockyard. Thomas Moon had come this way only once before in his life, and that was the time he'd looked her up to apologize and had felt like a king about it afterwards.

Now he felt like a toerag instead of a king. But something made him retrace his steps and knock on Mrs Innes's door. He knocked once, twice, three times. He didn't know what he'd say, or even if the door would ever open.

But suddenly it did.

"Yes?" Mrs Innes blinked.

101

An overfed ginger cat appeared on the step. It regarded Thomas Moon solemnly. Mrs Innes blinked. Thomas swallowed. The ginger cat stared at him balefully. Lots of things welled up that he wanted to say. But what came out was funny.

"*The Merchant of Venice* – I'm sorry – I didn't mean to – "

Mrs Innes was a middle-aged widow with dodgy eyesight. She remembered Thomas, of course. He seemed bigger now, but younger – and very upset, she could tell.

"Thomas," Mrs Innes said. "I thought we'd been through this."

"And I never would've done it if I'd known it was you – "

Thomas was strangely wound up, anyone could tell. *The quality of mercy* ... Mrs Carrier. He'd never see her again ... *is not strained*... Her funny smile. Her warm voice with its fascinating accent, reeling out *La Famille Delarge* ... *it droppeth* ... Her kindly footfall behind him, her unfailing help with French verbs, the way she ... *as the gentle rain from heaven* ... the way she – yes – *understood* him ... *upon the place beneath*...

"I wish it hadn't happened – and I wouldn't have – done it – if I'd *known*."

"Calm down. I know you wouldn't," Mrs Innes told Thomas gently. "Didn't your headmaster get the letter I wrote? Won't you come in?" she said.

Thomas shook his head. "I don't know about any letter. He never mentioned it. And my best teacher lost her job trying to stick up for me. And my best friend just moved away, so I'll never see *him* again, either. And I'm not clever at school like I told you, I'm crap and I sit at the front. And I daydream and don't even work, when I know astronauts have to study and stuff, and I don't want to *be* anything else – "

Thomas Moon took a deep breath. His voice sounded strange even to him.

" – and now I'm suspended till *September*, and I'll probably just have to work in a *supermarket* the rest of my life or something, because I always blow everything out. And my mum and dad, I feel guilty when they support me and I *want* to be like they want me to be, but I—"

"Thomas." Mrs Innes shook her head. "Thomas, Thomas, Thomas—"

"And at the theatre that time, I *wanted* to see the play, and I feel like *rubbish* at school and they think I'm a waste of space, when I *could* do the work if I wanted, it's just that I..."

"Just that you what?"

"It's just that I don't *want* to," Thomas finished, lamely. "I'm useless, that's all. They're right."

"You don't really believe that, do you?" Mrs Innes searched Thomas's eyes. "Why are you telling me this?"

"I want to be honest before lift-off," he found himself saying. How good it felt. "I want to be just what I am."

"And what's that?" Mrs Innes waited. She really wanted to know.

The words were framed before he was born, before he'd even grown into them. Delight in being *exactly what he was* and no more, no less, framed the name Thomas knew he would give himself.

"Well, Thomas Moon – who *are* you?"

"Me?"

"You could be anything."

Thomas Moon looked up and knew it. Planets swung in his eyes. Nebulas burst, white dwarfs condensed, cold moons of Jupiter beckoned – Callisto, Io, Europa...

Thomas spread his arms.

"Me? I'm *Mister Spaceman*."

Part Two

COUNTDOWN

```
Return-Path: <Thomas.Moon@gremlin.net
From: TCM24<Thomas.Moon@gremlin.net
To: Mint@Mint.ogre.co.uk
Date: Sun 12 Jun 11:07:03 GMTOBST
Subject: Mission Update
```

Mint,

In case you're wondering what I'm
doing, I'm hanging out with Adey
next door. Remember Adey next
door? Maybe you don't, he's a
first year. I probably wouldn't
hang out with Adey at all except
we're both off school till the
autumn, and there's nothing much
else to do. Adey's off school
because he got hit by a bus. He
spent for ever in hospital and now
he's supposed to be resting at
home, except his parents went back

to work and he's ticked off at
home on his own. Did I tell you
about Adey's dad?

Adey's dad's really scary. He'd
pop you one soon as look at you.
You don't want to meet him on the
path round the back of our terrace
unless you're mad. It's not even
like you could say hello. Even my
parents are scared of him. Poor
Adrian, Mum goes. Can't be much
fun with a dad like that. Too
right, Dad says. He's a nasty
piece of work, that Pugh. Have you
seen his eyes?

You should see Adey when his dad
calls him. ADRIAN. You can hear
Adey's dad three gardens away.
ADRIAN, WHERE ARE YOU? Old Adey
looks three times smaller. I got
to go, it's me dad.

It's good for Adey his dad works
long hours because just the sound
of his key in the door or the
sound of him coming up the path's
enough to scare anyone. I should
know, I catch the feeling off
Adey. Me, I stay out of the way
when Adey's dad comes out to get
coal from the bunker with his
sleeves rolled up and a shovel and

a face like a serial killer. But
you can feel him in Adey's house,
not that I go in there that much,
because Adey's too scared to let
me. At first I didn't see why.
Adey'd have something he had to
do, like record something his dad
wanted to watch, or take some
stuff up the launderette or get
some fags in for him, and he'd be
that desperate if something went
wrong, or he lost the money or
forgot it. I must be thick or
something. It took me a while to
realize Adey's scared of his dad.
I'm scared of Adey's dad. Just the
look of his shoes by the door's
enough. Just the sight of his fags
on the chair.
He's that hard, is Adey, you
wouldn't know he was scared. That's
how he got hit by the bus — playing
chicken in the road? Even his dad
went to visit him in hospital,
probably the reason he stayed in so
long. But that was ages ago. Me and
Adey, we're training together these
days. We did some EVA the other day
over Mrs Kingsley's garden? Mrs
Kingsley saw us. She waved a bit so
I gave her the A-OK. Then she comes

out and goes, Tom, is that you?
Would you like some runner beans
for your mother? Why are you wearing all those clothes?
You'd think she'd be freaked by
spacemen in her garden. She's all
right, Mrs Kingsley. We sat on the
bunkers a long time and I gave old
Adey debriefing. Adey's training
up pretty well. I may even give
him some simulator. I had a Rigorous Training Directive the other
day. We're officially into Countdown now. Countdown can last like,
weeks.
Better go now.
Does your mum go in your room?
Mine does. I'm getting a lock on
my door.
Mail me if it's not too much trouble. Now that we're into Rigorous
Training there may not be that
much time.
Yours from deep space
The Man in the Moon
Mail me if it's not too much trouble.

Thomas Moon hit SEND without much hope of a reply. The mysterious SPM29 was a better correspondent than Mint these days. Probably Mint never thought of him. Probably it might be time to remind him. Go to see him, even. Meanwhile, there was training to think about. Countdown had started, hadn't it? Time for some dedicated scheduling.

Taking his Landmarks in Space Exploration calendar down off his bedroom wall, Thomas Moon marked in the countdown all the long way down *June* and into

July

1	Tue	3	Canada Day (Can)
2	Wed	2	
3	Thu	1	
4	Fri	LIFT-OFF!!!	Independence Day (US)

in big red numbers, ending with LIFT OFF! on the Fourth of July. The Fourth of July was the launch date so far. But how would he really lift off? Where would his spacecraft be? Would someone come to fetch him? It might be a simulation, of course. He was ready, whatever it was. One day soon SPM29 might knock on his door and tell him *Well done* in a gravelly voice, and take him away in a plane, to a real space-training facility for end-training prior to launch. How would they know he'd prepared himself? Had he been spotted somehow? Who *was* it who knew his innermost dreams, the innermost reach of his heart?

IMPORTANT YOU LOG TRAINING HOURS, his last Directive had said. Thomas Moon ran over Order of Preparation in his mind:

The Stars (navigation)
The Simulator (communications, repairs,
    computers, boosters)
The Aircraft Loop
The Centrifuge
Weightless Environment Training Facility
    (WETF – underwater training)
The Spacesuit
Quarantine
Training Complete

That was the Training. His Mission: to orbit the earth and to do some experiments. He'd read a few books. But what could he actually tick off his list? What training hours had he logged? He'd been to the Gun Room a few times, sure, but WETF was lagging badly. He could possibly tick off navigation and maybe some simulator, but how about weightlessness training in the Aircraft Loop, or heaviness training in the Centrifuge? A fairground ride was the nearest he'd get to centrifuge training for simulation of rocket-launch pressures, and he could forget about the Aircraft Loop.

Where would he find a lightning-fast plane to take him up to loop the loop just so that he could be weightless for the few seconds the aircraft was falling?

Then there were Emergency Procedures. To go into space he had to be able to cope with fire, power failures and faulty parachutes, plus he had to be able to control all vital Life Support Systems, and what Life Support *wasn't* vital? And he had to learn all this with no help, because it was the dream of his life, and it seemed to be coming true. Or half-coming true. Or something.

If only he could win a place at the Euro Space Training School. Incredibly, this was a real place and they took cadets just like him, Thomas knew. He could hardly live with the knowledge and not be there. You could live and breathe space for a week. Live like an astronaut would. Practise launch simulations in a full-size mock-up of a spacecraft. Experience weightlessness on a moonwalk. Wear overalls with European Space Programme patches. Live the dream every day.

A week at the Euro Space School would look great on any CV. Thomas had read about it hungrily. Then it had started to hurt. The kids in the pictures at the Euro Space School website had looked unappreciative to Thomas. How did they get selected? They didn't know how lucky they were. He could do it better, he knew. Just give him half a chance.

Finally Thomas Moon hated them. Those kids were taking *his* place at Space Training School. His life-dream, *his* window of opportunity, *his* big break into space – were being taken by somebody else, probably someone who liked it the way you like the Black Hole Ride at a theme park, not *lived* it the way he did. He'd written off loads of times. Filled in application forms. Entered lucky draws and competitions. But no way would he get to France, which was where the Space School was.

Thoughtfully Thomas Moon replaced his Landmarks in Space Exploration calendar on his bedroom wall behind his bed. The red-numbered countdown put him suddenly back on schedule. If thinking about it wouldn't change things, *maybe seeing Mint would*. Thomas closed Pandora and opened Infonet. REQUESTING LUDLOW: SHORTEST RAIL JOURNEY? He initiated a Search for train times. In an instant they flickered up. Shortest Journey Time meant changes at Bristol and Newport. The ten-thirty train would be good. Mint would be gobsmacked to see him. But not too gobsmacked, he hoped.

Thomas felt unusually decisive. His life was changing, he could feel it. Already the long days with Adey had made him forget about school. Now he felt pointed and focused. Suppose a real astronaut was, in fact, mysteriously contacting him. Exciting, or what? Stranger things had happened. Helen Sharman knew.

Stranger things lived on the Net. Supposing he was searching for a secret way to contact someone, where would he look? Where did the mind of the Gremlin live? In the heart of installation procedures somewhere? Unlikely, Thomas thought. But he looked anyway:

```
PPP ENABLED
PPP driver          COM_2 Baud
Rate = 38400 Hardware handshaking
IP buffers = 32     Packet buffers
= 16
Auto login initiated
Executing script
c:\comms\gremlin\login.cmd
PPP DISABLED
```

– and on and on and on. It was fascinating. Like a foreign language. Screens and screens of computer script, all of it junk to anyone but a programmer. What did it all mean? And how could someone sneak in? *Send a message under another message,* like a shuttle slung under a rocket? Where did the Directives come from? From the mind of Gremlin Net, which had it in for him? From some other mind, somewhere? *Or could someone do it to themselves?*

Thomas Moon enjoyed pretending. Anyone

could pretend on the Net. That was the best thing about it. You could call yourself anything you wanted. You didn't have to be yourself. The weight of yourself was all gone. You could float as light as air on the Net and no one would bring you down.

```
Atz
OK
at & cl k3
OK
at lldt01752201707
CONNECT 38400
```

Installation script was for geeks. Thomas felt his head spin, and there was more:

```
User Access Verification
Username: Moon
Password: * * * * * *
PPP mode selected
Will try to negotiate IP address
Script completed
PPP ENABLED
My IP address = 193.164.150.59
```

Thomas shut down as soon as he could. PLEASE WAIT, said the screen. IT IS NOW SAFE TO TURN OFF YOUR COMPUTER. Thomas turned it off. Nothing like this would bring him closer to the mind of SPM29. SPM29 would reveal himself when he was ready and not before. Till

then he lurked in cyberspace, ▪
himself show, but not too much. Tho⌐
building up a picture already. Soon he woul⌐
know who he was.

A scraping sound under the window caught
his attention. Adey? It usually was. Thomas
had got used to Adey clambering up onto his
ground-floor bedroom windowsill and intro-
ducing his bullet head into the top part of his,
Thomas Moon's, open window. It was a big
window with top lights that opened, and it
wasn't a bad arrangement. It saved Adey ringing the front doorbell and Thomas having to
get out of bed to answer it on a sleepy late-
lie-in Saturday morning, and soon it had got
to be a habit. Adey always looked for him
there. But his dad gave him hell if he caught
him.

"Coming out?"

"Not right now."

"Come on," Adey wheedled, his bullet head
only just fitting through the opening part of
the window. "Please? Before my dad gets in?"

"What d'you want to do?"

"Rig'rous Training, what else?"

Thomas Moon turned to face Adey's
scarred knees, facing him through the
window. It was a compliment, in a way, that
Adey bothered to climb up and bug him. It
showed how much Adey wanted him that he'd
take a chance even *being* there, when his dad

might come home any minute. Or how bored he was. Poor Adey was half-starved for something to do. What was the *rest* of Adey's life like? And he thought *he* had a problem. Thomas considered Adey's knees. Then he said:

"Come in, please, Wayfinder Three."

"Wayfinder Three – we copy you. Over," Adey responded immediately, slipping happily into space-communications simulation. Wayfinder Three was the name of his service module.

"We copy your Rigorous Training Request." Thomas Moon considered. Was Adey ready for this? "We have a – Code Nine on this one."

"A Code Nine? Are you serious?" Adey looked at Thomas as well as he could through the top light. "We request you repeat your Code Nine."

"Affirmative, Wayfinder. You are Code Nine, repeat, you are Code Nine to Lift Off."

"We copy," Adey said, meekly. "Over and out." He withdrew his head from the window. "Dunno what my dad'll do."

"What's that?" Thomas called.

"My dad'll go mad if he finds out," Adey said.

"He won't find out though, will he?"

* * *

Long after his bedtime that night, Thomas

116

Moon earwagged in the corridor outside his parents' room. He often earwagged in the corridor when his parents were discussing his future. He learned quite a lot that way. But tonight the discussion was puzzling. More puzzling than any, so far.

"Expensive, but worth it, I'd say." – Dad

"How will we manage the fees?" – Mum

"I could do more overtime." – Dad

"You do too much already. Thomas and I hardly see you." – Mum

"What about the shop?" – Dad

"If the shop breaks even, I'll be surprised. There's Stannary Cards to pay. Then there's heating and lighting." – Mum

"We'll manage somehow. It's worth it, for Thomas." – Dad

"How much is it, per term?" – Mum

"If you need to ask, you can't afford it." – Dad

"Colin. I need to ask." – Mum

Colin. I need to ask. Silently Thomas Moon retreated back to his room. Whatever his parents were discussing, they might have asked him first. He might have saved them the trouble – a special-interest hobby, expensive lessons in something or other, the school ski-trip – camp – he would knock them all back, in any case. He wasn't interested in anything they might try to tempt him with to get him to work next term. They might as well not bother

117

asking him. Not that they asked him anyway.

When at last the discussion had subsided and his parents had gone to bed and the telly was cold, and the cold stars outside were beckoning, Thomas set out his kit. He checked his watch resentfully. T minus twenty minutes and counting. Could he help it if he wasn't in the mood? He would have to go now he'd said he would. Adey would be waiting.

Coldly Thomas Moon prepared for a Code Nine that night. Coldly he checked his food, his torch, his sleeping bag, procedures list, logbook, exercises. He would see what a Code Nine would do. Then he'd get WETF next week. Before that he'd email Mint, if Mint could be bothered to read it.

Coldly he called for Adey. Adey was waiting by the gate. He had a bottle and a hat and a blanket. Thomas Moon nodded and joined him.

"All right? Let's go if we're going."

Adey's face looked ghastly in the moonlight.

"What's the matter with you?" Thomas asked.

"When you come out just now, I thought you was me dad for a moment."

"Well, I wasn't, was I? Status?"

"We have an A-OK on your Code Nine tonight." Poor Adey seemed less than certain.

And no wonder. *Crimewatch* boomed behind the curtains in Adey's living-room.

Someone turned up the volume. Someone else turned it down. *"I'm not deaf!"* someone said. *"Get me another beer."*

"Come on, then," Thomas said, roughly. "We haven't got all night."

He couldn't quite forgive Adey tonight for not being Nicolas Mint. He wasn't in the mood for a Code Nine at all. But spacemen had duties, not moods. They had procedures and schedules and protocols. They never forgot their families, and called them on Father's Day. They kidded around quite a lot, but all their jokes had to be corny. And they never forgot a buddy. Poor Adey didn't count. He wasn't in the same buddy universe with Nicolas Mint. Thomas missed Mint badly. Spacemen had to have buddies. Without buddies, they couldn't get through.

Shouldering his rucksack, Thomas Moon set out for Golding's Hotel with his namesake moon silvering his back and poor old Wayfinder Three trailing along behind him, like a satellite trapped in his orbit. But he didn't need a satellite, no matter how friendly or obliging. What he needed, instead, was a brother. Thomas Moon would never have a brother. But right now a buddy would do.

"Keep up, can't you," he growled at Adey, "or we're never even going to get there."

Too soon for Thomas Moon, the dark bulk of Golding's showed them its shadowy back alleyways, its chimneys huffing chicken smells, its cheerfully clattering windows, gently steaming with gossip and laundry and all the breath and business of the world of a big hotel. Slipping in at the steely side door by the wheelie bins, they stormed the concrete stairs to Level 4. They paged the lift. Stepped in. No one saw them do it. Thomas threw the buttons all at once. The lift shuddered, grated, stopped. Thomas looked at Adey.

"A-OK," he said.

Adey sat down acceptingly. He got out his bottle and blanket. Then he took off his hat. He looked up at Thomas expectantly.

"Request instructions," he said. "This is Wayfinder Three. Mission Control, come in, please."

Thomas looked at Adey coldly. Mint would have known what to do. So would Barry or Neil, or anyone else his own age. Mint had gone away. Barry and Neil were useless, now more than ever, because they weren't supposed to collude during suspension, whatever *colluding* was. It sounded a bit like colliding in space. But the kind of space Thomas felt suspended in was a million miles from Barry or Tedious or Neil. Adey was suspended in it, too – but separately, inside his spacesuit, and Thomas Moon was inside *his*. That was how close they were. He would have to go through with the Code Nine now. But he didn't have to like it.

Thomas sat down next to Adey. "Free time, Wayfinder Three."

"What does that mean?" Adey said.

"It means shut down and be quiet. You know how to do that, don't you?"

Adey actually flinched.

"Sorry." All kinds of thoughts filled Thomas Moon's mind, including – even – the thought that Adey might just be scared of him. "It isn't even quiet in space. I don't know why I said that."

"What's so noisy?" Adey asked. He really wanted to know.

"You *think* it's quiet, but it isn't. You've got these fans, right? They circulate the oxygen in the space station? They're really noisy, but you have to have them, else you'd suffocate in *your own breath* – "

"Why would you?" asked Adey.

"Because the air you breathe out doesn't circulate, it just hangs around near your face. If you didn't have fans to move it, you'd breathe it back in again, right?"

"Right." Adey opened his bottle of Black-bird cider and began to perk up quite a bit.

He passed the bottle to Thomas Moon. Thomas Moon drank deeply. Might as well, before take-off. You couldn't drink properly in space. He passed it back and wiped his mouth.

"You have to wear earplugs at night," he

finished, "else the fans'd keep you awake. There's loads of other things, too. Like, you don't know which way is up."

"Why not?"

"Because," Thomas said, "how would you? There *is* no way up in orbit. You're falling towards the earth at twenty-nine thousand kilometres an hour, four hundred kilometres up, and there's no gravity, right? And your flight jacket's poppered onto your trousers, right, else it'd float up over your ears – "

"Why don't they wear dungarees?" Adey wanted to know.

"Because they just don't, that's all."

Thomas Moon frowned. Astronauts in dungarees. No one could be heroic in dungarees. How could Adey think it?

Somewhere in the depths of the Golding's kitchens, under-chefs clattered cutlery. The chambermaids were sleeping; the bar-staff had gone to bed. The great hotel slumbered. No one missed service lift B4 that much. No one cared that it had jammed, not even the astronauts inside it.

Thomas Moon stretched and yawned.

"Ready for launch, now?" he said.

"We copy your launch request," Adey said happily. "We have all systems go."

"On launch day you sit in your suit, and you check all your seals – "

"Check."

122

"We might wait two or three hours before launch, but we have to be suited up."

"Suited up," checked Adey.

Thomas Moon settled back against his rucksack. His voice took on a dreamy note. He really felt very tired. "And your seat's moulded to fit you, right – "

Adey wriggled and closed his eyes. "It fits me really well."

" – and there's no countdown in Russia – "

"Why not?"

"Because everyone knows what they're doing, countdowns are just for show – and the starter rockets fire – and the fuel's kerosene with liquid oxygen, and as the first stage ignites and the gases burn, they push us up and up – "

Adey felt the force.

"And as we go up and up we feel ourselves getting heavier – and heavier – three times as heavy – "

"I'm twenty-one stone," Adey panted.

"And you can hardly lift your arms to press the buttons – then BANG!"

Adey jumped.

"Final stage rocket is jettisoned and suddenly you're floating – "

Adey floated.

" – floating in your seat against your straps, else you'd float away."

Adey closed his eyes and floated away.

"And you look out of your window, and there's the earth – and the different colours of the ocean – "

Adey saw them all.

"And you orbit the earth *sixteen times* every twenty-four hours, so you get sixteen sunrises and sunsets *every day*, and you *never* get tired of seeing 'em – "

Adey knew he wouldn't.

Thomas Moon was good at spinning dreams. He looked at Adey, slipping away to sleep on a dream of space, and he knew that it was probably the biggest and best dream poor Adey would have, bar playing for Man United. Adey was all very well. He didn't panic or argue. He did what he was told. He'd be good in space, would Adey. But still, he wasn't Mint.

Thomas Moon closed his eyes. Alone from the first moment he swam, curled up, in a different kind of space inside his mother, he'd been extraordinary too long to make contact with anyone but someone who really knew him. Someone who could orbit Mister Spaceman and understand every side of him. Someone in radio contact no matter which stars blocked the signal.

There was no clear substitute for the real thing when you came down to it. You could whistle down the wind all you wanted. You could wish for the moon on a stick. When it came down to it, what he needed most – had to have – was Mint, Mint, Mint, Mint, Mint.

LIFT-OFF

Return-Path: <Mint@Mint.ogre.co.uk
From: Mint<Mint@Mint.ogre.co.uk
To: Thomas.Moon@gremlin.net
Date: Sun 12 Jun 19:30:52 GMTOBST
Subject: Quinlan Stinks
Hey, Moon-boy, guess what?
Quinlan only ruined my life. He
only wrote and told Miser Gaines
at Richard Robartes, my new school
here in Ludlow, I was up for that
bullying thing last year? Now just
because I smacked Billy Austen,
who rubbished me first to start
with, I'm on probation at school.
Thanks a lot, Mr Quinlan. I have
to sign in every lesson because
they have to know where I am every
second, in case I go mental or
something? I can't believe he did

```
it to me. He actually had to tell
them.
Miser Gaines says, It's up to me
now. Miser Gaines is my new head
teacher. He's so stingy we've got
no railings, no chairs, no books,
plus the bogs belong to the pri-
mary school next door and you
wouldn't send a dog to pee in
them, I'm not kidding.
Got to go.
Yours in hate & misery
Mint
```

Yours in hate & misery. Poor old Ludlow
Shropshire. Thomas rubbed the sleep from his
eyes and wrote a reply right away:

```
Return-Path: <Thomas.Moon@gremlin.net
From: TCM24<Thomas.Moon@gremlin.net
To: Mint@Mint.ogre.co.uk
Date: Mon 13 Jun 07:28:02 GMTOBST
Subject: See U Soon
Dear Ludlow Shropshire,
Sorry about your probation, it
stinks. Trust Quinlan to reach out
and nobble your chances, somewhere
they don't even know you. Did I
tell you Mrs Innes, the woman who
complained at the
theatre, said she wrote Quinlan a
```

letter so he wouldn't come down so
hard on me and Barry and Neil and
Tedious? He never even mentioned
it. He just suspended us anyway.
I thought about coming to see you.
So I thought I'd come today, hope
that's all right.
I'm feeling really tired this
morning. I only just got in. Adey
and me did this thing last night,
this Code Nine at Golding's Hotel?
A Code Nine's a night in the lift.
First I wasn't in the mood, but
then Adey had this cider, so we
drank it and practised launch pro-
tocol, cool! Adey's good in space.
He doesn't mind being shut up
alone, so long as his dad's not
around. He's been shut up alone
plenty of times. He doesn't mind
it at all. I don't mind it with
Adey. We make a pretty good team.
But then we fell asleep and never
meant to. Then this morning, these
cleaners get in. They're going,
Wakey, wakey. They see all our
stuff spread out, and then they
start going on. You haven't been
stuck here all night, they say.
That's terrible. You poor things.
You should complain to the man-

ager. That's all right, I said.
We're going now, aren't we, Adey?
So then we went, really quick. I'd
rather be stuck there a week than
have those chambermaids going on.
We got home about seven o'clock
and no one knew what we did. The
only thing is, sneaking back in
just now, I think Adey's dad might
have seen him. I hope he didn't
see him. Adey's in trouble if he
did. Now I'm worried for Adey.
Hope things turn out OK.
I'm really tired right now but I
should get some kip on the train.
I'm catching the ten forty-five.
It gets in at three-fifteen.
Did you know there's a place named
after you?
See you in Ludlow, Shropshire -
Over and out
T.C. Moon

It had sounded pretty easy. *I'm catching the ten forty-five. It gets in at three-fifteen.* But it hadn't been as simple as that. Thomas had left out the row he'd had with his mother. The row with his mother that had made him leave when he might not have actually gone through with it.

The morning hadn't panned out the way

he'd planned it, in those long hours in night Simulation. Plenty of things had gone wrong – beginning and ending, probably, with his being so tired that morning. Mistake number one, he'd fallen asleep almost as soon as he'd got in. He'd hung up his space-sleeping bag on its space-sleeping hook on the wall. Then he'd got in it for a moment. He hadn't meant to, of course. He'd meant to pack up and get off. But the sight of his sleeping bag drooping on its big brass hook in the wall had been just too tempting, in the end.

Thomas Moon had got used to sleeping upright. That was what spacemen did, only it didn't matter to spacemen which way up they were, because whichever way up, they were floating. Thomas Moon couldn't float. But it was surprising how soon you got used to it. So long as the hook kept you upright and you jammed your pillow under it and did up your drawstring tightly under your neck, like real spacemen did in space, to stop them floating out when they were fast asleep and drifting around bumping into things, it was scary how comfy it felt, even if you did rip your sleeping bag and end up on the floor quite a lot. You could sleep standing up just about anywhere. It was kind of a handy thing to know how to do.

And that wasn't the only thing. It was surprising how quickly you got used to eating out of tubes, as well. Thomas Moon had come to prefer them to almost anything except roast dinner and rich chocolate mousse. Dining from tubes was no problem, except for the range. He usually ate pesto or cream cheese, sandwich spread, pâté or apple sauce. You'd think someone might have noticed, but no one ever did. Thomas ate alone by the telly. His parents ate later, together, things that Thomas didn't like. Usually they drank some wine and talked in murmurs. Thomas had a burger much earlier. No one watched what he did. It was easy, ditching his dinners. Easy to take up eating from tubes. Easy to get to like them, so long as you had ice-cream after. Breakfast was usually yoghurt and jam. You got yoghurt and jam in space.

But he hadn't had breakfast that morning. He'd got in tired and cross. Left Adey by his back door. Climbed in by his own bedroom window. Flung down his things and checked his mail on computer. Looked for SPM29s and found Mint's email instead. Crisply left his reply. Hung up his bag and climbed into it. And had fallen asleep straight away.

The next thing he heard was his mother:

BAM! BAM!

"Thomas?"

BAM! BAM!

"Thomas – are you getting up today?"

BAM! BAM! BAM!

"Thomas! Open this door!"

With a tremendous exertion Mrs Moon forced open the bedroom door and squeezed her way in round the side of it. She scanned Thomas's bedroom confusedly. Then she felt the bed.

"Where are you, Tom? Are you there?"

"I'm here," Thomas husked. "Behind the door."

Thomas Moon's mother turned and saw the sleeping bag on the hook in the wall behind the door and her son's head lolling out of it. For a second all sorts of ghastly thoughts flashed instantly through her mind. *What d'you want that hook for? To hang things on, perhaps?*

"Thomas," she said, to the lolling head, "what on earth are you doing?"

"Sleeping standing up," the head returned.

"But why?"

"It's all right," Thomas soothed her. "It's only what astronauts do."

"No, Tom, it's not all right." Mrs Moon unhooked his sleeping bag and unzipped Thomas Moon. "This whole arrangement is dangerous. I don't want you in it again."

"But it's only a hook in the wall – "

"You really frightened me, then. This space-thing's gone far enough. It's not normal to sleep standing up."

"It's normal in a spacecraft."

"But you're not *in* a spacecraft, are you?"

"Aren't we?" Thomas Moon felt annoyed with himself. Annoyed that he'd fallen asleep. Annoyed that his mother had found him. "If I shut the door, how would you know?"

He pushed the door with his foot, and Mrs Moon saw that he was right. She might have been in some kind of spacecraft. The door closed flush with its silver surrounds. Even the mirror had been boxed in a silvered wall. Mrs Moon looked around. It was quite a long time since she'd come in and really *noticed* the way he'd been doing up his room. No wonder he spent so much time alone. It must have taken him ages.

"What's that?" she asked. Thomas's wardrobe was almost unrecognizable.

"Sleep station," Thomas told her. "Where the other astronauts sleep."

"The other astronauts?"

"Adey. When he stays."

"That boy." Mrs Moon shook her head over Adey. "Did you notice that mark on his neck?"

Thomas Moon had, but didn't say so. Something prevented him acknowledging Wayfinder Three's lumps and bruises. Had Adey got in all right that morning? The lights had been on in the Pughs' kitchen when he'd left Adey by his back door. Had Adey made it to his bedroom in time? Had Mr Pugh seen him come in?

"Well," Thomas said, "what do you think?"

"Not bad," Mrs Moon admitted, still taking in Thomas's room. Of course she'd noticed the silver paint going upstairs and the obsession with corrugated cardboard. But not what it had all added *up* to. She nodded again at his ingenuity. "Really not bad at all."

Thomas had a flair for artwork, Mrs Moon knew. Sometimes he did the shop window, and people always came in. The card shop was known for its windows. Once he'd done a sea scene with lobsters and green glass fishermen's floats and lengths of blue netting. In amongst all the netting, he'd arranged every card in the shop to do with a sea scene. It had really brought people in. They still came in to admire the wall-length parchment he'd written in Olde English script, listing every wedding anniversary and the stone – or wood, or china – they were celebrated with.

But he'd really outdone himself this time. Mrs Moon looked around and took it all in, not picking up socks or shorts or straightening the bed, but really seeing what he'd done. He'd gone to a lot of trouble to get the look absolutely right. The control panels looked so real – at least, she imagined that they did. From the look of the poster on the wall – Inside the Mir Space Station – there could be little doubt that Thomas had done up his room, using anything he could get his hands on, to look *as much like a space station interior as possible*. He'd even used the platform over his bunk-bed to mock up a flight-deck platform. Loads of chipboard and dowling. *Bombs* of silver paint.

"I like it," she said. "I like it a lot. Who did the woodwork – you?"

Thomas nodded. "It's old wood from under Dad's workbench."

"Where did you get the control panels?"

"Sent off for 'em – good, aren't they? They're only vinyl overlays."

"Sent off for them, where?"

"The Euro Space School in France? They do loads of stuff like that."

"It's really something, Thomas, except – " A shadow crossed Mrs Moon's face. "I wouldn't actually mind, except – "

"Except?"

"The sleeping behind the door," Mrs Moon almost whispered.

"It's not that weird."

"Yes, it is."

"You didn't have to come in."

"I wanted to tell you something."

"You might've asked me instead of just breaking in."

"I did knock."

"I was asleep, all right?"

"Behind the door. On a hook in the wall."

"I always end up on the floor. Don't make

135

it such a big deal."

"You've been up here for days on your own."

"And?"

"You haven't done any *work*. You haven't even opened these books Mrs Carrier sent you."

"I have done work, actually. I've done work I want to do."

"What work?"

"Work for joining an astronaut programme some day."

"Oh, Thomas, *please* grow up."

"Don't you realize? Can't you *see*? I've got things I want to do. Now I'm suspended I'm doing them – and *you're* not going to stop me."

"Yes, I see that now." Thomas Moon's mother stared at him. "The space thing's really important to you, isn't it?"

"I've only been telling you *for ever*."

"I had no idea you took all this so seriously."

"Oh," Thomas said, "and now you do?"

Thomas Moon's mother sat down on the bed. When she looked up at him again worried lines stood in her face. "Would you like a new school in the autumn? Your dad and I think it might help."

"I'm sorry?"

"A new school," Mrs Moon repeated.

"Somewhere to make a fresh start."

"You think a new *school* might help?" *Come in, Control, we have a problem.*

"Somewhere like Box College. Your dad and I have discussed it, and we're going to see it next week – "

"*Box College? Excuse me?*"

"Mr Braintree – he's the head teacher – said to come and look round before term ends, so we can, well, you know – get the *feel* of the place."

Box College. So that was it. Thomas Moon flashed back on his parents' discussion. *How much is it per term? If you need to ask, you can't afford it. Colin, I need to ask.* It all made sense now – and how. No wonder they never asked him.

"You might've *asked* me," he said, breathless with the outrage of it all, unable, yet, to grasp what they'd done – might do – to him. *Space Station Moon to Control. Help me. Please come in.*

"You haven't been happy, have you?" Mrs Moon's voice had a steady edge, as though she'd made up her mind. "You didn't deserve to be suspended, your dad and I know that. You need a new start, a chance to shine, then you can put it behind you. Those others are such a bad influence. Mr Braintree understood straight away."

"I can't believe I'm hearing this." *Mission*

Control – emergency – do you read? "I get suspended, Mint's up in Shropshire, I have no friends, my best teacher's gone – and you want me to start a *new school*?"

"Well – " Mrs Moon seemed nervous. "We thought you might like the idea."

"Well, I don't, I hate it, what did you think?" *We have a Code Red, do you copy?* "Did you even *think* about asking me?" Thomas was white-hot with anger. "Did you think I *wanted* no friends? Is that what you thought when you did it?"

"Of course not, we simply— "

"What did you think, it's *easy*, starting again?"

"I know you've had a few schools now, but— "

"I've done it so often I should know, right?"

"It's a good school, Tom – we're thinking of you."

Thomas snorted. "I don't *think* so."

"We want you to be happy. To do the best that you can. You want that too, don't you?"

Thomas Moon stared at his mother. All communications were down. *Emergency contained. Over and out.* Already he'd decided what to do.

"I'm getting dressed now, all right?"

"But you're dressed already."

"What if I am?" Of course he was – still dressed from the Code Nine last night. "What

138

if I am? Can you just go? Can you just leave me *alone*?"

Later that day Thomas Moon boarded the two forty-five train to Bristol Temple Meads exactly twenty-nine minutes late. The train had been delayed due to signal failures down the line. Thomas Moon himself had been delayed by missing the morning train entirely.

It didn't bother him much. Not even borrowing his mother's Mastercard and coolly ordering a train ticket to Ludlow over the phone in a Mrs Moon-type voice bothered Mister Spaceman these days. Spacemen had clear objectives. Mission imperatives were paramount, whatever paramount was. His ticket had arrived three days ago. Super Saver Single, it said. He would have to look at least sixteen.

As Thomas flashed along on the train to Bristol Temple Meads – he liked the sound of *Bristol Temple Meads* but would only change trains there – back at home his mother got in and viewed his room with dismay.

"Thomas? I've got a surprise! Tom – where are you – are you there?"

The discarded rucksack in the middle of the floor was sufficiently unlike Thomas to make Mrs Moon pick it up. She held it and knew absolutely. Thomas had gone somewhere.

He'd been upset – that row this morning. She picked up a T-shirt and sniffed it. If he hadn't taken this rucksack, he must have taken the other. Checking the flight-deck above the bed, Mrs Moon noticed straight away that Thomas's Adidas rucksack was missing. He'd gone somewhere with his rucksack and a few days' underwear.

It was then that she noticed the calendar. Landmarks in Space Exploration. A count-down had been carefully numbered in red throughout June – and *July* – to LIFT-OFF! on the fourth. What did it mean, Mission Count-down? Why were all the days numbered? Countdown to what? Why were they heading towards LIFT-OFF!

And in any case, LIFT-OFF! *where*?

Thomas Moon flashed along on the train from Bristol to Newport. He would change at New-port for Ludlow. What a long time it took to get to Ludlow. What a lot of changes. It was a bit like a three-stage rocket bound for the moon. Already stage one had been jettisoned. Now for a stage-two burn.

And the ticket collector.

"Tickets, please," the man in green said. "Tickets from Bristol, please."

We have a – Code Red here. Thomas Moon ran through it in his head. *Travelling far, sonny? You've got an Adult Single here.*

140

Thomas practised widening his eyes. *Does it matter? I'm meeting my mum. I don't know why that is.*

"Tickets, please. I thank you."

The ticket collector drew nearer. A woman over the way offered him her ticket. The ticket collector glanced at it briefly – thank you – then moved along the aisle. Thomas's heart jumped in its cage. He prepared to look at least sixteen.

"Your tickets from Bristol, please."

Thomas held out his ticket. He knew he looked totally adult. Never doubt it, my man. But the ticket collector hardly looked at him. He glanced at Thomas's ticket and then moved on, looking and asking for tickets, looking and asking for tickets, until he was gone.

Thomas Moon deflated. So. *We have a – Situation Green.*

"I *wish* Thomas hadn't gone out," Mrs Moon was telling Adey at home. "I just booked tickets for a surprise holiday, and now— "

"Can he come out tonight?" Adey asked her stolidly, in the kitchen.

"When he comes back, but I'm worried he's gone somewhere. He seems to have taken his rucksack." Mrs Moon considered Adey. "You don't know where he's gone?"

"I know he was doing lift-off. We've been doing lift-off for ages."

"Adey – what *is* this lift-off?"

"*Space* Station lift-off." Adey grew bored. "Will he be out after tea?"

"Adey? Where's he gone?" Mrs Moon gripped Adey's shoulders. "Just a minute – keep still – what's that mark on your face?"

Adey shrugged. "My dad."

"He hit you? Why?"

"'Cos I been out all night."

"Where?"

"Doin' a Code Nine."

"A Code Nine?" Anxiety seized Mrs Moon. She gripped Adey's shoulders harder, revealing the livid bruise under the neck of his T-shirt. "Adey, where's Thomas gone? Adey – lift your shirt up – did your *dad* do *that* to you?"

INTO ORBIT

Here am I
Sitting in a tin can
Far above the world
Planet earth is blue
And there's nothing
I can do...

                – David Bowie, "Space Oddity"

```
Return-Path: <Thomas@Mint.ogre.co.uk
From: TCM24<Thomas@Mint.ogre.co.uk
To: CTMoon@gremlin.net
Date: Tue 14 Jun 12:30:15 GMTOBST
Subject: Sorry
Dad,
Please don't be angry. I meant to
say sorry yesterday, but when I
rang Mum she got upset. Can you
tell her sorry from me? I know it
was stupid to run off to Mint's,
```

but I thought you wouldn't worry
if I rang you, and I did ring,
didn't I? Please tell Mum I didn't
go because of the argument. I
wanted to see Mint anyway. But now
I'm not sure why.
Mint's been acting weird since I
came. I don't think he wants me to
be here. It's funny how you think
you know someone, then you find
out you don't? Tomorrow we're
going bowling, then after that
we're seeing a film. It's not the
same with Mint any more, but at
least now I know it isn't, so I
won't be wondering what he's doing
any more, because he's doing the
same as me. Or the same things we
used to do, when I was going to
school, except now he does everything with Drew. Drew Parsons,
great name or what? Drew goes
everywhere Mint does. No way can
you get rid of him. He comes round
all the time.
I can't even talk to Mint these
days. This morning I'm getting
dressed and he goes, You're mad,
you are. Just because my toothbrush
is tied to my sleeve. I had to
explain about weightless conditions

in spacecraft again. What does he
think, I'm making this stuff up? He
doesn't seem to realize you have to
tie things down all the time else
they float off and clog up the air
filters. It's good to get in the
habit of doing it. Then, if you're
ever in a spacecraft, you won't
even have to think about it.
Thanks for letting me stay. I'll
mail you after the film. Mint's in
school, anyway, so there's not
much point me being here.
Love, Thomas
PS Did I tell you about the
Americans on the train?
PPS How upset is Mum on a scale
of one to ten?
****

Return-Path: <CTMoon@gremlin.net
From: Dad<CTMoon@gremlin.net
To: Thomas@Mint.ogre.co.uk
Date: Tue 14 Jun 17:45:46 GMTOBST
Subject: Collecting You Sunday
Dear Thomas,
Of course your mother's upset. But
at least now she knows where you
are. We'll have to talk about it.
NEVER do that again or your life
will be shorter by two or three

years, like ours. I hope you enjoy
a few days with Nicolas. I didn't
know you missed him so much. I'm
sorry it's not quite the same, but
of course people change with time.
I've spoken with Harry and Viv,
and the long and the short of it
is, I'm coming up to get you on
Sunday. Mum says it's Box College
next day, so we need to get you
back pretty smartly. Mum isn't too
pleased with you and neither am I,
but there it is, it's done now.
She wonders how you found the
money to get up to Shropshire on
the train. I'm wondering too. No
doubt all will become clear.
Keep out of mischief till Sunday.
Love, Dad
PS It's a funny thing, but the
Incoming Messages list has a
number of unexplained TEXT files
attached. If I didn't know better
I'd have said someone's been doing
something pretty complex without
quite understanding how to do it.
It's a mystery!
****

Return-Path: <Thomas@Mint.ogre.co.uk
From: Thomas<Thomas@Mint.ogre.co.uk

To: CTMoon@gremlin.net
Date: Wed 15 Jun 11:05:53 GMTOBST
Subject: Drew Parsons Is an Alien
Dear Dad,
Thanks for your email last night.
Tonight we went swimming, cool,
except Drew Parsons came too. I
hate Drew Parsons. You would too,
if you saw him. There's got to be
an alien inside his head working
his face with levers.

Tell Mum she'd like Ludlow a lot.
The houses all look like the Dutch
Oven tearooms in town, all black
and white and leaning and stuff,
really old and quaint, but there
isn't that much to do except visit
the castle. Mint goes over to
Drew's house a lot. Viv makes him
ask me if I want to go too, but
I'd rather lick out an EVA suit
after a three-hour sweat-and-weld.
Just kidding. I'd rather eat toenail clippings.

Mint would rather eat toenail
clippings than hear me talk about
space. Did I tell you about the
Americans on the train? On the
train coming up to Ludlow, these
two big American guys get on with
these two big cases and ask for

Here-ford. DOES THIS TRAIN RUN TO
HERE-FORD? The conductor goes,
Herryford, not Here-ford. Everyone's laughing, including me. But
they sit down right next to me
anyway, and guess what, they're
talking spacecraft. I can't
believe what they're saying.
They're talking clean rooms, here.
10K cancellations of contract.
Sterile boxes and containers. One
guy goes: So I said to Helen, no
kidding — would you use that for
spacecraft?
So I had to ask them. Excuse me, I
go, excuse me, did you say spacecraft? What, are you working for
NASA? Did you go into space? I
must have been drooling or something. They look at me like I lost
it. Then one of them goes: We man-
ufacture medical equipment. We're
here for a trade convention. After
a while they move seats. Would you
excuse us, they say. Thank you.
Have a nice day. It's obvious they
think I'm a valve short of full
integrity.
I told Mint about the Americans on
the train because I'm sure they
were covering up. Bet they work

148

```
for NASA, with their big square
suitcases and shoulders. But Mint
gave me that look, and maybe he's
right, I don't know. I think
things up so much, I'm not sure
what's real any more.
Do I have to see my new school?
See you soon.
Love, Thomas
```

Sunday, his father arrived. Thomas Moon parted the curtains at Mint's. *Dad*. Dad, pulling up outside. Dad jumping out of the car. Testily pocketing his keys and appraising the house. Dad, with all that *that* meant. Lots of things to do with home rushed in on Thomas Moon. He knew what he'd run away from the moment he heard the doorbell.

His father came in and drank tea. His bags had been packed since ten o'clock that morning, so there was nothing for Thomas to do but wait for the exchange of news and pleasantries to subside. Then he would have to get into the car with his father, and listen to what his father *really* had to say. He glanced at Vivian Mint, willing her to keep the conversation going. She smiled at him and asked after his mother.

"How's Lyn?" she asked Thomas's dad.

"Busy as always." Mr Moon shrugged through his biscuit.

Mrs Mint turned to Mint.

"It's been nice having Thomas – hasn't it, Nick?"

Mint swallowed and nodded. "Sure."

Mrs Mint turned to Thomas, sorry for him now.

"Come again any time, won't you?"

"Only next time, can you let us know?" Mr Moon put in acidly. He drank his tea, then added, "We like to know when he's running away. Then we can rent out his room."

At last the conversation washed on to something less dangerous. Thomas Moon met Mint's eyes. *It's been nice having Thomas, hasn't it, Nick? Sure.* He hadn't put himself out, then. *Sure* was such a little word, squeezed out like a pat of anchovy paste on a gleaming white spaceman's dinner tray. *Sure, it's been totally average.* Had that mean little *sure* been really all Mint could squeeze out? Thomas downed a couple of Jaffa Cakes. Then it was time to go.

Mint said goodbye outside. It wasn't a long goodbye. In fact, it was probably the shortest goodbye in history.

"Bye then, Tommo," Mint mumbled.

"See you," Thomas said. "Maybe when you visit?"

"Maybe." Mint nodded and smiled. "Flying low today."

"Oh." Thomas did up his flies. He looked

up, beetroot red.

A flash of Mint's old smile showed. "Remember what Smartie used to say? You won't get far in space with your shirt hanging out of your trousers?"

"You'd remember that, wouldn't you?"

"It was funny. You used to go red."

"And you didn't, Mr Get-Me-a-Polo Mint?"

"Not as red as you. *No one* could go as red as you."

"It's good you're pointing it out. It's not going to make me feel worse."

Mint actually grinned like he used to.

"Later, you man in the moon."

"Much later, Mint-with-the-Hole."

It could have been all right, as goodbyes go. But Drew Parsons lurked in the background. He actually lurked right behind Mint. No respecter of friendly goodbyes, he couldn't wait to ruin this one.

"I'm ready, let's go," Thomas Moon told his father. "Thanks a lot, Harry and Viv."

"No problem, Thomas. Safe journey."

Settling on his nose the aviator sunglasses that Thomas disliked so much, Mr Moon pulled away. One street followed another. Soon the town gave way to slip-roads and countryside. Thomas felt numb inside. He settled back in his seat. Nothing to do but *think* for three or four hours. He popped in a tape, then ejected it. The tapes his father kept in the car made him feel ill the minute he put them on, he'd heard them so many times. Plus he hated them to start with. Silence was better than music you hated. Even an awkward silence.

The motorway unfolded relentlessly. Had his visit to Ludlow been real? In no time Ludlow, Shropshire, was only a vaguely edged memory of white and black stooping houses. Thomas Moon felt number still. What was he going back to? He looked at his father, tense as usual. Why didn't he *say* anything? The silence between them ticked in the vein in his father's neck. It lived in his aviator sunglasses. They really were *so* sixties ... if *only* he'd take them off...

Suddenly Mr Moon said, "This was a bright idea."

"What was?"

"Dragging me up to Ludlow, the day before an important conference."

"Sorry."

"You might think of other people sometimes. The world doesn't revolve around you, you know."

"I know it doesn't."

"You need to get it through your head."

Thomas flushed. "I could've taken the train."

"You could've not gone without asking."

"It was only a training run."

"What for?"

152

"For when I'm, you know, an adult. For when I have a *life*."

His heart thumping, Thomas looked out of the window. Something resentful had woken in his chest already. *Thanks for coming and fetching me, Dad, when I never asked you to anyway. So I won't bother feeling grateful or saying thank you. Message aborted. Out.*

At Gambledene Motorway Services Thomas had a hot chocolate and the All Day Breakfast, which was fried bread, bacon, eggs, beans, mushrooms and tomatoes, sausages optional. Thomas Moon opted for sausages. Then he ate everything quickly and looked around. Everyone else chatted pleasantly with the people they were sitting with. Everyone knew where they were and what they were doing.

Mr Moon ate Ocean Pie seriously. Then he said, "You'll see your new school tomorrow."

"What?" Thomas looked blank.

Mr Moon cleared his mouth of puff pastry. "New school tomorrow," he repeated.

"Oh."

"Sorry I can't be there. Exterior Cladding Conference. Didn't realize it clashed."

Thomas couldn't find anything to say. He paddled the remains of his hot chocolate around with his spoon.

"Should be good," his father told him brightly. "At least you can see what it's like."

"Yeah, right," Thomas said. "I can see I

don't want to *go* there."

"It's a chance to look round with your mother and meet Mr Braintree. It's a good school. Brilliant results. Could do a lot for you, Thomas."

Yeah, right, Thomas thought. *And I could do a lot for it. Like never darken its doors with my whole life-disaster-thing.*

"Don't write it off before you've seen it," coaxed his father. "Tell Mum you'll give it a go. She's been worried sick about you lately."

His mother had worried more about him than Thomas Moon had dreamed. Meeting him at the door with anxious arms and even more anxious enquiries, the strain of the last few days stood in her voice.

"What time did you leave? Much traffic? Was it a tiring drive? How are Viv and Harry? Would you like something to eat?"

"About two o'clock. Yes, Mum. No, Mum. Fine, Mum. No, I had the All Day Breakfast." Thomas Moon hugged his mother again. She was good to get back to. Good to smell. Almost good enough to eat.

"Thomas – I've been so worried – Adey said you'd gone off on some kind of *space* game."

"I just really wanted Mint. I thought I'd ring you when I got there, and then you'd know where I was."

"You won't ever do it again, will you?" His

mother searched his eyes for Thomas's promise. "Run off like that, without saying?"

"Never." Thomas Moon meant it. "I never will, I'm sorry."

He looked around. The hall had swapped its dull beige wallpaper for a swingeing shade of purple. Purple paint ran over everything – the hatstand, the postbox inside the front door – even over the meter box. "I like the hall," he said. "But should you have painted the meter?"

Later, after a shower and a bit of unpacking, Thomas Moon moonwalked downstairs. He remembered to take off his shoes to traverse the living-room carpet. His mother looked up. She patted the sofa beside her. Thomas sat down and for quite some time watched *Dr Quin, Medicine Woman* in a warm glow of togetherness with his mother.

"How's the shop?" he asked.

"New lines in," said Mrs Moon. "And I'm ordering for Christmas."

"Christmas cards *already*?"

"You have to look ahead."

When *Dr Quin* finished, Mrs Moon got up.

"Ravioli all right?" she asked Thomas.

"Can't I have a burger?"

"It's home-made," Mrs Moon said. "I thought we'd eat together, for once."

"Can't I have a sandwich or something?"

155

"Thomas."

"Sorry. I'm not very hungry."

Saying as little as possible was going to be their best way around this, Thomas Moon knew. Eating together was the last thing they needed to do. The tension between his father and himself was bad enough already. His parents, he knew, were waiting for some explanation, some way to hold on to what they thought they all had together as a family, which was a different thing to what they actually had. The tension grew worse as Thomas watched telly while his mother fiercely heated dinner. He felt like the main course himself. He tried to eat, but couldn't. Not even toasted sandwich.

The coast was clear. Ducking into the kitchen, Thomas flipped open the bin.

"Why aren't you eating?" his mother demanded.

Thomas spun round. He hadn't seen her come in.

"I am." Surprised in the act of binning his toasted sandwich, he flushed a deep shade of beetroot. "It's just, I'd rather eat space food."

"Space food?"

"Things in tubes."

Mrs Moon put some crockery away. Then she straightened suddenly. "I've got a surprise for you."

Thomas waited, annoyed with himself. Why

had he mentioned space food? He should've just said he wasn't hungry. That was what he usually said.

"I was saving it for after dinner," Mrs Moon went on, "but – "

"What?"

"Well, it's nice to have it now."

The surprise, Mrs Moon explained, her voice becoming less certain as she went on, *was a holiday in America*. To Disney World, if he liked. He'd like that, wouldn't he?

"Maybe." Thomas brushed past her coldly. "I'm not a kid, you know."

"Well, thanks, Mum. Thanks a lot," Mrs Moon said sarcastically. "Don't bother getting excited or anything." She appealed to his father on the settee. "Did you hear what he said? If this is what Nicolas Mint's done, I wish he'd never—"

"What's that about Mint?" Thomas shouted outside.

"I said, *If this is what Nicolas Mint's done, I wish you'd never been to see him.*"

"It's nothing to *do* with Mint. I don't *care* what Mint does any more. I have got a *brain*, you know."

Thomas entered flight-deck in his bedroom. *Requesting flight-deck clearance. We have a Code Red here. We copy your Code Red. Flight-deck clearance granted.* Then he flopped down on his bed. He felt worse than

157

ever. A holiday in America. Like he *deserved* a holiday in America. They'd probably even take him to Houston, if he asked them. Spoilt, spoilt, spoilt, spoilt, spoilt, spoilt, *spoilt*.

Spoilt, and now without Mint. He had got a brain. And he *did* care about Mint. But their flight paths diverged, and that was that. That was the way it was, in space. He'd had to let go of Nicolas Mint, and he'd done it. Meanwhile, there were voices downstairs:

"Where did he get the money for the train ticket? That's what I'd like to know." – Dad

Thomas got up to close his door. He ear-wagged briefly in the corridor.

"Oh, I expect he saved up." – Mum

"Saved up, my hat. I'm going in to ask him."
– Dad

Once you let go of someone in space there was no turning back, not ever. One slip, a broken tether, and you floated on for ever till something else altered your course. Nothing could turn you back the way you came. Not friendship, not mothers, not anything. On and on you sailed till your oxygen ran out and your helmet and suit were empty except for a human-shaped prune. And still you went on, into deepest space, completely alone for ever, except for the stars. The stars were your only friends. Like friends, they could never reach you. You could only float between them.

The spaceman's parents talked on in the

living-room.

"Leave it, Col. I'll ask him tomorrow."

"But I—"

"Leave it. I'll find out tomorrow."

Thomas Moon returned to his room and sealed the spacecraft door. Then he returned to flight-deck and composed himself in his bunk. A tumbling spaceman. Falling forever into the furthest reaches of the universe. It was a lonely thought, but one which wouldn't leave him. He turned out the light and the stars winked coldly beyond his window, the same stars that winked over Mint – the same but not-the-same Mint he'd thought he knew so well.

For a moment he pictured the old Mint, in a flash of remembered episodes. Then he put the pictures away. An astronaut didn't complain. *We regret your divergent flight path, but have set new co-ordinates. Commencing lone space flight now. Good luck. Over and out.*

He was on his own. It was Sunday, June 19th. T minus two weeks and counting.

Monday, Mint went back to school. And so did Thomas Moon.

SPACE STATION
H.E.L.P.

Box College was an imposing red-brick building that didn't do itself any favours. Neither did Mr Braintree, the equally imposing head teacher. Both looked self-important. Both expected high standards. Both looked as though they were made of red brick, which one of them was, and one of them wasn't. Both looked as though they had had a lot of money spent on them, which both of them actually had.

First Mr Braintree imposed on Thomas's mother.

"Come in, Mrs Moon. Won't you sit down? I hope you won't mind my asking, but could you remove your shoes?"

"My shoes?"

"So sorry. New parquet."

Thomas finally got it by studying the floor while they talked. The floor was made of new wood tiles. Braintree didn't want them pitted by his mother's high-heeled shoes. Shoes she'd bought specially to see him in. At least they weren't red, or worse, white.

After Mr Braintree had imposed on his mother, he imposed on Thomas Moon – *in the nicest possible way*.

"So. Thomas. What do we say?"

Thomas was nonplussed. "Sorry?"

"The problem is," his mother put in, "Thomas has a rather overactive imagination. That's been the problem up to now."

"We prefer to talk about *predilections*, not problems." Mr Braintree smiled intelligently. "Here at Box we make something of a speciality of square pegs in round holes. Shall we tour the laboratories? Mrs Moon? This way."

Predilections – what were they? Did he have many of them? Were they good or bad? Thomas tried to remember to ask his mother. Braintree had called him a square peg in a round hole, which rankled a bit and made Thomas Moon pull back his hand from the door rather than risk any contact with Braintree's. But he soon forgot his annoyance in the tour round the halls of Box College. He forgot about predilections. He even forgot to be self-conscious. He forgot about everything.

Never had he seen so many plant-filled reception rooms, so many well-equipped classrooms, so many dwindling corridors smelling of polish, so many endless turns through double doors. How *big* was Box College, anyway?

"This is the atrium. We encourage reading here." The sun beamed in on Mr Braintree's head through the glass-covered atrium roof. "As you'll see," Mr Braintree went on, "the space is defined by a notional boundary dividing it from the library and the computer room. It's a calm space for reading and for exchanging the news of the day."

"It's lovely, isn't it, Thomas?" Mrs Moon was impressed.

"Yes," Thomas said, "it is," imagining Barry and Neil and Tedious exchanging the news of the day in its notional boundaries. "Must get a bit noisy for reading."

"Audio-baffle tiles." Mr Braintree slapped the wall. "Soaks up local sound."

"Oh," Thomas said, "right." He'd thought local sound was a radio station. Braintree was worse than Quinlan. He spoke in some kind of decorator's code probably only his mother would understand.

Mrs Moon went on ahead with Mr Braintree, squeaking at murals and oddly placed sculptures, unusual alcoves with corkboards, non-slip corridor tiles, the wooden-clad dining hall, the sweep of the central stairs. It had to be her dream morning. Thomas followed glumly, deep in thought.

They passed extensive art rooms. A glossy

gym. Laboratories dripping with equipment. A hall like the United Nations Assembly. In a paved area outside, a swimming pool swashed queasily under its solar blanket. Beyond the swimming pool, well-tended sports fields rolled away to a prosperous avenue of trees. Everything looked sleek. Well-oiled. Complacent. Even the students ran on wheels.

End of period caught up with them in Foster-Bailey Wing, which was, Mr Braintree assured them, entirely given over to The Arts. As the bell rang the students filed out in an orderly fashion. Mr Braintree joined his fingers as they went. "They, ah – have two minutes to relocate. Timetabling permitting, of course."

Of course. Thomas watched the unhurried change of lessons. The Boxers swished smartly past with their books. In the darkened corridor, they didn't seem real, somehow. No one carried a rucksack or a coat or jostled or pushed or joked. They actually had a locker each, and all their uniform matched. All the girls had their hair tied up, and all of them seemed to be blonde. All the boys had their ties done up, and everyone gave way to everyone else and nobody seemed to rush. In moments the corridor had cleared. It wasn't a bit like end of period at Boundary Road Community School. No pushing or bombing or scabbing a seat ahead of everyone else, or shouting *Hey,*

163

Not like his own tutor-group. Thomas watched the last Boxers joylessly departing around the corner. Probably they were looking forward to exchanging the news of the day in the atrium. Probably they were aliens in disguise. He hoped they went wild round the corner. Once out of sight, they would – wouldn't they – be *real*, like anyone else?

At last the tour came to an end. Back at reception, under a display entitled "Environmental Threats to Our Rural Landscape", Mr Braintree stood too close to Thomas and said, "Well, Thomas, what do we think?"

With an effort Thomas didn't say, What do we think about *what*? because more was required of him that day. In the end, he said, "Thank you, Mr Braintree." It seemed a safe thing to say.

"Thank *you*, Thomas Moon." Mr Braintree extended his hand. With horror, Thomas had to grasp it. "It's not every day we meet new challenges." Mr Braintree dropped Thomas's hand like a dead thing almost as soon as he took it. Then, "Mrs Moon," he said, warmly, clasping both Thomas's mother's hands in his.

Thomas Moon waited while Mr Braintree took his mother's hands for considerably longer than he'd taken his, Thomas Moon's – like he was sorry.

Mrs Moon couldn't say enough. "So good

of you, Mr Braintree. Thank you for showing us round. We're really both very impressed. I'm sure he'll be very – of course we will. Goodbye for now. And thank you." Thomas wished she would stop.

At last they could walk away. All down the long gravel drive he considered his feet. But once beyond the Box College gates, with their pompous cast-iron curls, Thomas Moon turned on his mother.

"You didn't have to say all *that*."

"All what?" Mrs Moon said mildly, still in a dream of dining-hall tiles and gleaming glass tables in reception.

"All that thank-you stuff. I thought you were never going to *stop*."

"Well. People remember your name if you thank them a lot, you know."

Thomas Moon hoped Mr Braintree would forget his name instantly. He could still feel the pressure of Braintree's hand; the way he'd dropped his, Thomas's, hand like a dirty wrapper or a thing he didn't need any more. The way he'd held his mother's hand too long. The strangely hushed alien Boxers in the corridor came back to haunt him on the bus home; the weird way the oily Boxers had filtered past Braintree in silence. He might be completely off his head, but Quinlan was a star beside Braintree and his hushed and lifeless Boxers. If that was what Box College wanted, Thomas thought, they could box him out for ever. Even if it was the best sports hall he'd ever seen in his life.

They sat on the bus in silence. In silence, they walked the lanes home. "Lovely school," murmured Mrs Moon. "Lovely, lovely school."

"Mmm," said Thomas Moon. Then he said, "Who's that, in Adey's gate?"

Bodger Daniels, the music teacher. Going in at Adey's gate. Up to Adey's front door. Disappearing inside. Thomas's brain worked overtime. *Adey? And a* music *teacher?*

Aloud, he said, "He must be taking lessons."

Despite himself, he recalled the Pughs' front room. Dark and dank and depressing, it had all the terrifying overtones of the rest of the house, except – it had a piano. And a picture of Mrs Pugh playing one. The piano and the picture above it were the only things in the house not filled with dread. Thomas thought about Mrs Pugh. Mrs Pugh had had blonde hair once. She'd even looked pretty in the picture. Before she'd got tired and battered-looking. Maybe she'd once had a life. Maybe she wanted one for Adey.

"Adey? Taking *music* lessons?" Mrs Moon broke out laughing. "That'd be a turn-up for the books."

"He couldn't be, could he?" Thomas said. "Must be some mistake."

It seemed so ridiculous. Adey. With his broken knees and his dropped aitches and his complete disregard for anything not a football.

But why would they have Bodger Daniels?

Unless – someone was *learning piano*?

"Adey *is* having lessons. I just spoke to him outside."

Mrs Moon smiled. "Oh, no."

"He's got to practise every day, or else."

"So it's "Chopsticks" for ever, now, is it?"

"His mum says he's got to improve himself. His dad says he'll kill him if he doesn't."

"Oh, right. Good incentive. That'd make anyone play."

Thomas Moon met his mother's eyes. She got things wrong sometimes, but he really, really liked her. Not everyone *liked* their mother. But Thomas Moon was lucky.

"Tom, about Box College – "

"Can we talk about it later, when Dad gets in?"

Thomas Moon kissed his mother, not entirely to head off trouble. Then he escaped before the mood could change. He felt lucky and safe. At least his parents listened – usually – to what he had to say. At least they weren't like Adey's. At least he didn't have to take *piano* lessons. He pictured Adey thumping up and down the keyboard with his bitten nails, his battle-scarred legs pumping pedals, his bullet head nodding in time. He'd have to learn to read music. Practise *scales* – no way. He'd be out of the window in no time. They'd have to nail him down.

Still picturing Adey escaping, Thomas flipped on the computer to check his mail. He opened Mail/New Mail. His mood of optimism was rewarded by a congratulatory *Bing!*

YOU HAVE NEW MAIL! enthused the Mailbox.

Mint, you beauty. Thomas Moon entered and waited.

But nothing could have prepared him for the email that popped up onscreen:

```
Return-Path: <BoundaryRd@BoundaryRd.
ac.uk
From:
LMCBoundaryRd@BoundaryRd.ac.uk
To: Thomas.Moon@gremlin.net
Date: Mon 20 Jun 10:31:02 GMTOBST
Subject: Happy Holidays!
Dear Thomas,
Hi, it's Louise Carrier. I was
wondering how you are, and how
you're getting on with your
French. I'm using the school com-
puter. I found your address in the
Penpals Mailbox, I hope it's OK to
use it. I'm not very good at
email!
```

168

```
School breaks up in three days, so
I hope to have a good, long holi-
day. I'm going to France this
year. Who am I kidding, we go
every year! We never get tired of
Brittany. I hope you are off on
holiday, too. Wherever you go,
have fun.
You can reach me at home at
Louise.Carrier@ogre.co.uk
I hope we stay in touch.
Best wishes,
Mrs Carrier
```

Best wishes, Mrs Carrier. But earlier, she'd
said Louise. *Hi, it's Louise Carrier.* And she'd
bothered emailing from school. She'd thought
about him *that* much, despite – well, despite
everything. Thomas Moon could picture the
library computer. He could picture Mrs Carrier sitting at it. He'd sat at it often, himself.
Added his address to the Mailbox under Pen-
pals: Special Interest: Space. That was the way
she'd found it. It was good for him that she
had.

Thomas replied right away:

```
Return-Path: <Thomas.Moon@gremlin.net
From: TCM24<Thomas.Moon@gremlin.net
To: Louise.Carrier@ogre.co.uk
Date: Mon 20 Jun 16:46:38 GMTOBST
```

Subject: Thanks for your Message
Dear -

Dear who? Thomas paused. What should he put? *Louise Carrier? Mrs Carrier? Louise?*

Dear Mrs Carrier,
Thanks for your email, it really
surprised me. I hope we stay in
touch, too. I hope you enjoy your
holiday. My mum wants to go on
holiday, but I don't want to go.
I mean, I do want to go, except
she wants to go to Disney World
and I'd rather go to the Euro
Space Centre in France, I guess
you know why.
Today Mum and me visited Box College. It's really nice except that
I hate it. Please try to come back
to school next term, it won't be
the same without you. Mint hates
his school, as well. Mr Quinlan
wrote to Mint's new head teacher.
Now Mint's new head teacher hates
him. I went up to see him, but
Mint's changed a lot. Now he likes
Drew Parsons. Drew Parsons is nerd
of your life.
I went back to see Mrs Innes again
— the lady in the theatre I said
sorry to? She's really surprised
her letter didn't come up at the

```
Governors' meeting. It might have
made all the diff.
I'm doing some French now and
then. I worked out what the French
is for We Have Ignition and We
Copy Your Problem and Rocket,
except I've forgotten them now.
Things haven't been going so well,
but they might be going to get
better. At least I hope they are.
With –
```
Thomas paused again.

Warmest Regards? Sincerest faithfulness? Major-time respect?

```
With best wishes,
Thomas Moon
```

Double-clicking SEND, Thomas Moon sat back. He hoped his email would sit in Louise Carrier's mailbox and pop up onscreen at home when she'd cooked some dinner and opened French wine and sat down. Her email from school had gone out to him today. His was going out to her now. She could reply anytime. She might even –

Bing!

YOU HAVE NEW MAIL! The familiar box appeared onscreen.

I'm sorry? Thomas blinked.

She must have read his message right away. *The incoming mail was from Louise Carrier.* All it said was:

```
Return-Path: <Louise.Carrier@ogre.co.uk
From: Louise<Louise.Carrier@ogre.co.uk
To: Thomas.Moon@gremlin.net
Date: Mon 20 Jun 16:48:13 GMTOBST
Subject: What Letter?
Thomas,
WHAT LETTER?
Louise
```

Thomas, what letter? She must be sitting at
her computer at home. Thomas felt embarrassed. This was *too* direct. He'd better reply
right away. What did she mean, What letter?
It took him a moment to think.

```
Return-Path: <Thomas.Moon@gremlin.net
From: Thomas<Thomas.Moon@gremlin.net
To: Louise.Carrier@ogre.co.uk
Date: Mon 20 Jun 16:49:05 GMTOBST
Subject: Your Message
```

Dear — Louise? The way she'd signed herself?
Dear Louise – no, he couldn't.
```
Dear Mrs Carrier,
The letter from Mrs Innes, you
mean? You know I told you I went
to see her? Well, Mrs Innes wrote
this letter to Mr Quinlan saying
she accepted our apology, and
```

172

would he drop the matter. That's
what she told me she said. She
thought Mr Quinlan might read it
out at the Governors' meeting, so
then they might not hammer me and
Neil and Baz and Tedious. But Mum
said he never said a thing. I
thought he might have told you he
got it. I thought he might have
told me.
My dad just got in, so I better
go. He's been to an Exterior
Cladding Conference in Birmingham
today. That's what he sells, Exterior Cladding, except I still
don't know what it is.
Au revoir,
Sincerely best wishes from
Thomas

"Dad!"

"What?"

"Is that you?"

"No, it's Mission Control from Houston!
They've sent me to sign you up!"

Thomas Moon shut down and joined his
father.

"Dad. Don't joke about that."

Mr Moon set down a bag carrying the
legend CLADDING FOR THE FUTURE. Crowning
Thomas Moon with a paper baseball hat

which also said CLADDING FOR THE FUTURE, he set it at a jaunty angle on his son's head and grinned. "Everyone had these on backwards, even the managing director. You had to've been there," he added, when Thomas made a face.

Thomas took off his hat and looked at it. "Dad – there's something I've been wanting to ask you – "

Mr Moon looked meaningfully at Mrs Moon. "Oh," he said, "what's that?"

"What is exterior cladding?"

Throwing a number of whistles, balloons, Biros – and other freebies – at Thomas Moon, Mr Moon sat down and enjoyed his cup of tea. Cladding, he explained, as Thomas very well knew, was any surface material on a building, including aluminium, timber, slate, vinyl, but most especially uPVC fascias, soffits and bargeboards, in brown woodgrain effect, or classic white if you wanted. A soffit, he added sternly, sealed in the space underneath the eaves of a roof, in case Thomas had been about to ask.

But Thomas hadn't. Instead, he said, "Guess what? Adey's having piano lessons."

"You're kidding me."

"It's true," said Mrs Moon. "We saw Mr Daniels call in."

"Mr Daniels?"

"Music teacher. Used to teach at the school.

Lives over the junk shop down the road."

"Him," nodded Mr Moon. "Always wears the same clothes."

"Adey says he's coming twice a week, and his dad says he's got to practise every day. Or else," added Thomas, darkly.

"Adey. Playing piano." Mr Moon started to laugh. He set down his cup of tea. "I'm sorry, I just can't picture it. He's not the sensitive type."

"He soon will be," Mrs Moon said. "If his father has anything to do with it."

"What do they say, you can't make a silk purse out of a sow's ear?"

"That's not fair."

"But true." Mr Moon shook his head over Adey. "So how did you get on today?"

"Colin, you should have seen it. Such a lovely school."

"So – " Mr Moon turned to Thomas – "so, you like Box College."

"I didn't say that," Thomas stalled.

"And Mr Braintree – what's he like?"

Thomas searched for something neutral to say.

"He's got a new wooden floor in his office."

"And?"

"An ay-tree-um and a computer room. And they all have lockers, as well."

"So would you like to go there?"

"Not really, no thanks, I wouldn't."

Mrs Moon turned. "But Thomas – I thought you liked it."

"I did, but I don't want to *go* there."

"Why not?"

"Because."

"But *why,* because," Mrs Moon persisted.

"I want to go back to school. I don't want to run away."

"But this isn't running away. And anyway, you've *got* to."

"I've been to too many new schools."

"I'm afraid we've told Mr Braintree you're starting September the ninth."

"*What?*"

"We're getting the uniform next week."

Suddenly Thomas crumpled. He covered his face with his arms.

"Come on, old son, it'll be all right," Colin Moon encouraged. "Things aren't as bad as they seem. Everyone leaves school sometime, I remember I—"

"Thomas, come here." His mother stretched out her arms to hug him. "We only want what's best."

"Leave me alone. Don't *touch* me."

"That old school isn't any good for you. You'll do so much better once you've moved."

"Leave me alone, I said."

Thomas blocked both of them out. *Entering pre-flight quarantine. Contact with relatives terminated.* Backing away, he flung himself

176

out of the room.

"Where are you going? Thomas!"

"Out, like you even want to *know*."

Rushing blindly towards the front door, Thomas Moon flung it open. A callow-looking man in a suit stood outside, his right hand raised to knock.

"Oh!" Thomas stared.

"Would Mr and Mrs Moon live here?"

Thomas nodded dumbly.

"You would be – Thomas Moon? Are your parents in? Can we just step inside?"

Thomas Moon nodded dumbly again. His mother answered the door – "Ah! Mrs Moon?" and the man in the suit came in. He looked pretty young to be important. Only a few years older than Thomas. He still had a bad spot problem. Worse than the spots was his glossy manner, about as sincere, Thomas thought, as the glitz on the front of Golding's, when what lay behind was kitchens and steaming back stairs.

"Richard Tillson, Assistant Manager." He extended his hand with a smile. "Mr Moon. *Mrs* Moon. I'm from Golding's Hotel. It's about your son, I'm afraid."

"From Golding's Hotel?" Mr Moon shook hands, confused.

"That's right. I'm sorry to have to tell you that Thomas has been trespassing on hotel property. On quite a regular basis, I'm afraid."

"Thomas – trespassing?"

"A member of staff reported the matter. Not soon enough, I'm afraid."

"You're not as afraid as I am. Thomas – is this true?"

Thomas Moon shrugged and swallowed. "I went in the lift a few times."

"More than just a few, I think." Young Richard Tillson brought out a list. "And you did rather more than go in. Maintenance records show a calculated programme of vandalism. Service lifts B4 and B5 show regular jamming between floors from the first occasion on the eighth of May to a recent event on the—"

"Never mind the dates." Mrs Moon caught Thomas's shoulders. "Have you been doing this, Thomas?"

Thomas twisted away from her. *Quarantine violated*.

"Me and Adey did it. But we never damaged the lifts."

"How could you do this?" Mrs Moon shook Thomas hard. "After all this other trouble. I want to know. How-could-you-do-this-to-us?"

"All right, Lyn, calm down. You – over there." Mr Moon pointed to a chair and Thomas Moon sat down in it. Mr Moon turned to Mr Tillson. "I'm afraid this is a terrible shock."

Richard Tillson was afraid again, too. He was afraid, this time, that Thomas might not appreciate what a dangerous thing he'd done. Jamming lifts could go horribly wrong. He might be trapped for hours. This time it would be a caution. But should there be any repetition, which Mr Moon had assured him there wouldn't be, he was afraid – he was *very* afraid – that the Golding's chain would press charges.

After Richard Tillson had gone, Mrs Moon sat down hysterically.

Thomas stood tragically in the doorway.

Mr Moon put the kettle on.

"Well," he said, "Thomas. You continue to surprise us. What were you *doing* in the lifts?"

"Ber-ber-later."

"What?"

"Simulator," Thomas said, louder.

"What's that when it's at home? Some kind of silly space game, I suppose."

Thomas shrugged. He couldn't care what he said now. He couldn't be bothered to try to explain. No one would understand anyway. They didn't want to understand. They didn't care what he thought. *Shut the pod doors, Hal. Approaching Space Station H.E.L.P.*

"Well," his father said again, "consider yourself well and truly *grounded*, Mr High-Flying Spaceman, Mr I-Want-to-Be-an-Astro-naut-and-I-Don't-Care-*Who*-I-Hurt-in-the-

Process – "

Mrs Moon got up. She ran her hands through her hair, streaked, Thomas noticed, with grey.

"That's it," she said, "I can't take any more. We're going on holiday next week, *whether Thomas wants to or not.*"

Thomas found Adey outside on the wall. He hauled up beside him and after long moments when neither of them said anything, said, "Life sucks."

"Doesn't it."

"And after it does *that*, it sucks some more."

"Tell me about it," Adey said. "You don't have to do *scales*."

"No," Thomas said, "I have to have Richard Tillson from Golding's coming round, telling my dad I vandalized the lift."

Adey looked at him. "Bet you copped it."

"I did."

No one spoke for a while.

Then Adey said, "He's not coming round our house, is he?"

"No," Thomas said, "I don't think so."

Neither of them spoke for a long time. Finally Thomas said, "I'm going away, anyway."

"*Adrian!*" The bull-roar of Mr Pugh sounded around the houses.

"But I'll be back soon."

"ADRIAN!" – louder, this time.

"So I'll see you when I get back."

Adey nodded sadly. "We have a Code Twelve on this one."

"A Code Twelve?"

Adey nodded again. "Every man for himself. You got to look out for number one."

"*ADRIAN! WHERE ARE YOU, BOY?*"

Adey slipped down off the wall. "I got to go, it's me dad."

Thomas Moon watched Adey trailing off down the path, the most reluctant piano player in the world, and also the most overlooked. There was something pathetic about the way he walked. Something dejected in his shoulders.

Thomas felt like calling him back for a space game. It wasn't too late. Not yet. *Come in Wayfinder Three, Wayfinder Three, do you copy?*

But Adey had turned the corner. *Quarantine complete.* Thomas Moon couldn't help wondering how long it would be before he'd sight the bullet head of Wayfinder Three in his spacestation window once again.

HOMESICK – DO YOU HAVE A PROBLEM?

Return-Path: <Thomas.Moon@gremlin.net
From: TCM24<Thomas.Moon@gremlin.net
To: Mint@Mint.ogre.co.uk
Date: Wed 6 Jul 15:28:07 GMTOBST
Subject: We Have Lift-off
Yo, Mint!
We have lift-off! I'm not even at
Thomas.Moon@gremlin.net! I'm actually at moon dot having dot the
most dot fun dot intheusa dot!!!!!
Lucky Dad brought his laptop. It
means I can keep you posted, so
squirm when you hear what I did. I
actually visited space-camp, Tuesday, on a Day Pass? It was OK, not
great, a bit young. I like America
a lot more than I thought I would,
and I thought I would only a bit.
But the flight over was the best.

I ended up going on the flight-
deck, that's really next to the
pilot, really six miles high,
really over the Atlantic at four
hundred and eighty-two miles per
hour!!! Sharp end, or what? I
still can't believe I did it. You
should've been there. Mum asked
this steward. She goes, Is a visit
to the cockpit possible? My son,
he's interested in flying. She
actually said cockpit. Nobody says
cockpit. The steward was pretty
nice about it. Let me take your
son's name, he says. Then later he
comes back and says, Thomas Moon?
Let's go. We went through Business
Class and up this spiral staircase
and onto the flight-deck, coo-wol!
Up on the flight-deck, it's really
like, cramped. Just like a space
station flight-deck. The Captain's
on the left, yeah, then there's
the co-pilot next to the Captain,
and behind the co-pilot, there's
the engineer. Plus all these
switches and dials, you can't
imagine. So the Captain goes, OK.
Now we're on autopilot. This is a
Boeing 747 with four Pratt and
Whitney engines. See the horizon

there on that dial? It gives us
our orientation.
He shows me all the instruments.
So then I ask him some questions.
All the time we're in the nose of
this plane travelling at about
five hundred miles an hour. You
can't see a thing through the windows. He shows me where we are on
the map. The engineer watches
these dials. Fuel Consumption,
most of them say. He watches them
all like mad.
So after the Captain explains we
have three onboard computers, I
go, So, how d'you know when something goes wrong? With all these
dials, I mean?
When something goes wrong? I'll
show you. The Captain turns to the
co-pilot. When you're ready,
Stephen, he goes. Can we have a
Warning Lights Drill?
No, I go, let's not — let's not do
anything weird.
Next thing you know, it's a Warning Lights Drill. It isn't so bad,
but the flight-deck lights up like
a Christmas tree and every light
goes on. Then all the lights go
off again, and that's good, except

for the ones that are meant to be
on. And that's the end of the
drill.
Then the Captain says, Better go.
I think there's someone else to
see us.
There isn't, but I go back to Mum.
Did you like that, she goes? I
don't even know how to tell her.
Did I ever. So cool.
When we land there's this band
playing in the airport, "The Star
Spangled Banner", and everyone's
watching and stuff. They've got
flags, balloons, the works. Then I
realize, thick or what? It's actu-
ally the Fourth of July.
I actually had lift-off on the
Fourth of July.
Just like SPM29 said I would.
I never even noticed the date we
took off.
Spooky, or what?
Smell you across the Atlantic,
Thomas C. Moon, Junior
PS Did you know they eat different
dinners? The Captain and the co-
pilot? In case one gets sick to
his stomach and crashes the plane?
What if the engineer gets sick?
Who's going to watch the fuel?

```
**********************************
```

Return-Path: <Mint.@Mint.ogre.co.uk
From: Mint<Mint@Mint.ogre.co.uk
To: Thomas.Moon@gremlin.net
Date: Sun 10 Jul 11:03:49 GMTOBST
Subject: Tar-tar Drew Parsons

Hey, Moon-boy,

Ludlow here. You might want to
hear I stuffed up with Drew Parsons, big time. We went to the
beach, right? It only took all day
to get there and it wasn't the
greatest beach ever, plus I came
back with tar on my Nikes, but how
was I to know? I'm supposed to be
sleeping over, but Drew Parsons's
mother goes ballistic. That tar,
she goes, it's everywhere. You've
walked it all over the house. It's
even on Grandma's new tuffet.
I left pretty soon after that.
Drew never noticed I went. Next
day when I asked him for the money
he owes me, he told me I owed him!
I can see his point of view. The
tar got all over his bedroom. It
got on the dog. It even got in his
music centre and over all his
clothes. But what am I going to
do, apologize the rest of my life?

186

He can stick some tar in it himself, he just about makes me sick. So we haven't hung out too much. It wasn't really the tar. You can have enough of Drew Parsons. Tell me more American stuff. The flight sounds cool, I'm green. Get this — Mrs Carrier emailed me. She actually wrote to Miser Gaines. She told him I got picked on first, so don't write me off as a bully. "Nicolas Mint was victimized by a small group of boys and only retaliated. This doesn't excuse his behaviour, but neither does it merit supervision." That's what she told me she said. I don't know what Gaines'll say. She went to see Mrs Innes, too. She's on about some letter Mrs Innes wrote? She said to say she'll contact you soon, so don't say I never told you. Mrs Carrier's cool. Mum says I can come and stay with you sometime. Can I come and stay with you sometime? When do you get back? When I went to the beach with the Parsons sad sack I wished it had been us at Whitesands. Remember when we went to Whitesands

that time and buried Clint and
almost killed him?
Yours from Parsons-free Shropshire,
Ludders

****

Return-Path: <Thomas.Moon@gremlin.net
From: TCM24<Thomas.Moon@gremlin.net
To: Mint@Mint.ogre.co.uk
Date: Wed 13 Jul 09:38:04 GMTOBST
Subject: MONSTA TRUX
Yo, Ludders,
I think I destroyed Dad's laptop.
What happens is, when I boot up, I
get this little grey box.
The first time it came up, it
said: Warning! Your Crash Defender
program will expire in twenty-
three days. That was four days
ago. Now it says: Warning! Your
Crash Defender program will expire
in nineteen days. What happens
after nineteen days? Every day
it's less. It's really making me
nervous. I haven't told Dad yet.
Yesterday we went to this stadium,
about forty minutes' drive, and
saw MONSTA JAM WORLD TOUR!!! What
MONSTA JAM WORLD TOUR is, is these
excellent GIANT trucks on wheels
the size of houses. They have

188

names like Crypt Kicker, Rip It
Up, Krusher, Snake Byte and
Gravedigger, also Dragonslayer,
Executioner and Extreme Overkill.
What Monsta Trux do is jump over
cars, about six at a time, and
it's a race? They run on alcohol,
Dad says — about a gallon every
three minutes. When they turn up
the revs under those babies it
feels like your ears'll burst.
They're up the ramp the second the
start guy lowers his hand, you can
hardly stand to hear them, then
it's a flying death leap over six
cars, then majestic crash-
landings, cool! Gravedigger did
his axles in. That was him out of
the race. Last race was Extreme
Overkill v. Krusher. Everyone
wanted the Overkill. But in the
end Krusher took him.
Everything here's so cool.
Wish you could see it too.
Moonie
PS I just got mail from Tedious!!
****

Return-Path: <Thomas.Moon@gremlin.net
From: TCM24<Thomas.Moon@gremlin.net
To: Tettios.Taverna@ogre.co.uk

Date: Wed 13 Jul 09:52:02 GMTOBST
Subject: The Big Apple
Tedious,
Thanks for reminding me, like I
want to remember when school
starts. See you there on September
the 9th. I'm not going anywhere
else, so they better get used to
it, right? Big news before we came
away was, Mum and Dad think I'm
going to Box College. Box College.
As if. Not if I have anything to
do with it. They can't make me go
to Box College. It does have a
cool sports hall. But that's about
all it has cool.
America's really cool. We went to
New York on the bus. We walked all
around Times Square and went in
Macy's, then we took the Circle
Line Boat Tour round Manhattan
Island and under the Statue of
Liberty, then we went up the
Empire State Building and finished
up in Central Park. I love New
York. It's a happening city.
We nearly didn't get here. We were
going to go to Florida, except I
didn't want to. Mum wants me to
just relax and not worry about
anything, so guess what, I'm just

relaxing and not worrying about
anything.
Except for Box College, of course.
Gonna see you in school as usual,
or not gonna see you at all,
Over and out,
The Moon Boy
****

Return-Path: <Louise.Carrier@ogre.co.uk
From:Louise<Louise.Carrier@ogre.co.uk
To: Thomas.Moon@gremlin.net
Date: Thu 14 Jul 18:49:51 GMTOBST
Subject: See You Soon
Thomas,
I've been in touch with Nicolas
Mint. He tells me you're having a
wonderful time in America. I told
him I'd contact you soon. I've
been to see Mrs Innes. Mrs Innes
has a lot to say about you, and in
case you're worried, all of it's
good!
There are a few things in the
pipeline I'd better not mention
yet.
Have the holiday of your life,
Thomas.
See you soon,
Louise
****

Return-Path: <Thomas.Moon@gremlin.net

From: TCM24<Thomas.Moon@gremlin.net

To: Louise.Carrier@ogre.co.uk

Date: Sat 16 Jul 20:34:42 GMTOBST

Subject: Overlook Trail

Mrs Carrier,

Thanks for your message. Can you
tell Mrs Innes I'm sending her a
postcard? Thanks.

Today we went to Lake Condor. Lake
Condor's this massive theme park.
I went on every ride until I got
sick. I didn't get sick until the
end. I'm keeping a diary of things
we do at the Euro Space School
website, at:

EuroSpace@SpaceEd.ac.Fran

if you want to see what I've been
doing. They're running a competi-
tion. Write into Space — Win a
Week As a Space Commando. The
best three reports about anything
win a week at the Space Centre,
cool! Second prize gets a model
shuttle. Guess which I'm going
for.

Yesterday we climbed a mountain.
It was the highest point for
miles. The signs said Overlook
Trail and No Fires and Bear Coun-

try. We didn't see any bears, but
all the time we climbed you could
hear weird birds. Right at the top
we sat on this rock. All around
was this sea of trees, like nothing you ever saw before. Trees
right out to the horizon. It made
me feel pretty small. On the trail
back down again, I felt like the
Last of the Mohicans. I felt like
anything could happen. Like we
were on a raid. Jogging through
woods with our bows and arrows
with some heavy-looking Hurons on
our tail. I'm ducking and diving
through trees. Mum goes, Why are
you walking like that? Are those
trousers uncomfortable?
That was the Overlook Trail.
Mainly it overlooked trees. Mint
would've liked it, specially if
we'd seen bears. Adey would, too.
Adey's my next-door neighbour. He
got hit by a bus last autumn. His
parents just got him a piano
teacher, but if you ever saw Adey,
you'd know he's not the piano-
playing type.
I miss being at home quite a lot.
Sometimes I lie in bed and it's
like, I can see myself from space?

I'm alone on this huge great
continent with only my mum and
dad. I feel like no one can reach
me. But I feel that way at home.
I think I'm feeling homesick.
Monday week we climb in the big
bird and fly back home! Hope
they're showing good movies. I
flicked between channels and
watched two at once on the way
over. Also I went on the flight-
deck and met the Captain. Tell you
about it when I get back.
Message ends.
Thomas Moon

Part Three

SPACEWALK

The blazer was green and gold. It fitted uncomfortably closely, but the assistant was sure it was right. "That's the one," she said. "You don't want them baggy-fit. Box College doesn't like it."

Box College doesn't like it. Thomas Moon felt so depressed at the sight of himself in the green and gold blazer in the long fitting-room mirror in Speakes Menswear Department, he could hardly be bothered enough to care. Never mind what *I* like, he thought. *Hostile territory all around. Identity crisis ahead.*

Mrs Moon was all brisk decisions. The two weeks since getting back from holiday had been filled with misery for Thomas Moon. His transformation into a Boxer seemed to require all kinds of humiliating experiences. First he had to have hideous new shoes – two great black duds that sat on his feet like Bibles, reminding him where they would carry him, and why, at every deeply uncool step. Then he had to have The Haircut. The Haircut of Death would confirm his new-boy status anywhere he went. Talk about standing out. He might as well lisp and be done with it.

His mother never even noticed how badly he felt. Or if she did, she never showed it. Thomas Moon watched her bitterly. Look at her now, shaking out shirts at the counter. Comparing ties with the assistant. She was actually enjoying herself.

It wasn't as if he wanted to go back to school. Thomas Moon regarded himself sadly. What did he look like? It was just that, if he did go back, he wanted to go to Boundary Road. Boundary Road wasn't so bad. For a moment, Thomas Moon projected himself back at his desk in school. The desk he'd had before he'd been moved so often for dreaming out of the window. He pictured himself working hard. Swotting and learning. Shooting up his hand. Answering questions in class. Being handed back essays in a glow of accumulating praise. The dream expanded to include thunderous prize days with standing ovations. Quinlan bowing and scraping. Mrs Carrier smiling tenderly, her heart bursting with pride. It could happen. Why not?

"Hey, Moonie, what's new?"

Thomas Moon woke up. "Hey. What are

you doing here?"

Tedious shrugged. "Games kit. So when did you get back?"

He took in Thomas Moon in his blazer. He couldn't look away.

"We got back the twenty-sixth."

"How was it?"

"The best."

"Cool."

Thomas Moon shifted uncomfortably.

"That's it, then," Tedious said, "the uniform for Box College?"

Tedious wasn't snide. Philip Tettios was basically a nice person. But even he was struggling, Thomas could tell.

Thomas nodded numbly. The miserable boy with the knobbly knees nodded back at him from the mirror.

"You have to wear *short trousers*?" Tedious quavered.

"Only up to Year Eleven. Then you get Privileged Dress."

"Privileged Dress."

"Right."

Poor old Moonie. With an effort, Tedious kept it straight. He checked the mirror sympathetically. Wearing that blazer. How hard was *that*? Something passed between Tedious and the miserable boy in the mirror.

"You can hack it," Tedious said. "You can do it, Moonie."

"I don't want to," Thomas said. "I want to come back to school."

Tedious swallowed and nodded.

"'Luck," he said. And walked away.

Thomas Moon watched his own reactions in the mirror. The boy in the green and gold blazer looked back at him pathetically. What a loser. Even the Boxers would know it. He didn't look like a Boxer. He didn't look like a spaceman. He looked like nothing on earth. Could he *be* any goofier or lonelier?

"That looks really nice." Mrs Moon bustled up with an armful of regulation sweaters. She appreciated the blazer. "Really nice. How does it feel?"

"Wear it yourself if you like it so much," Thomas mumbled.

But his mother was on her shopping high. She didn't care how it felt. "Was that Philip Tettios? Why does he get his hair cut like that? It looks as though he's had an accident with that line round the side of his head. The assistant says these sweaters are smaller than you think. Can you try this one – and this one. Oh, and here's the tie. You have to tie it properly. Thomas? Are you listening?"

She loaded Thomas with sweaters. Thomas took them numbly.

"We'll get a satchel in Leathergoods. They stipulate a satchel. Then we'll pick up underwear in – Thomas – are you *crying*?"

*   *   *

Sunday lunch was a golden, contented, *family* meal taken in the kitchen, which overlooked the Pughs' back door. All the kitchens jutted out at the back of the terrace, one reason serial-killer Pugh's path to work lay past the Moons' back door. It was a right of way for the terrace. A right even Black Pugh had.

Black Pugh was the name Thomas gave him, whenever he thought about Adey at home, and his scowling father getting coal from the shed, which he tried extra hard not to do. It was way too romantic a name for a thug. But Thomas didn't dwell on it much. Sunday lunch was one of the few times he and his parents felt like a family. He wanted to enjoy it.

"Wonder where Adey is," he wondered aloud.

"Haven't seen him since we got back," his father said. "Heard him practising a few times. Poor kid struggles on."

"His piano?" Mrs Moon laughed. "He plonks away every day. He's certainly very determined."

"He's afraid for his life," Thomas said.

"Come on, Thomas, gravy?"

"No."

"How about some cabbage?"

"I don't want cabbage," Thomas said. "You said I didn't have to."

His mother set her jaw. "You'll have just a

little," she said, heaping some onto his plate.

Thomas scraped it to one side. He squeezed more Alpine Spread into his mouth. Then he ate some potatoes. He had to have potatoes. His mother had insisted. The rest he could eat out of tubes. If that was what he wanted.

"You'll get anorexic, you will," Mr Moon observed.

"Why can't you leave me alone? I'm not doing *you* any harm."

"Now then, Thomas," his mother said. "We're on your side, you know."

Thomas blinked. "You are?"

"Of course we are," his father said. "We want to see you happy."

"Then why are you making me go to Box College?"

"Box College is a very good school."

"Except I don't want to *go* there."

"You're throwing away a very good chance. A very good chance, indeed."

"I don't care, I'm not going to go!"

"All right, Thomas," his father said. "We'll talk about this later."

"There's nothing to talk *about*."

"Because you're fine."

"That's right."

"And you sleep on a hook in the wall. And you think about space all the time."

"I like space and I *want* to think about space – "

"You've been thinking about it too much. It's not negotiable, Thomas."

"What isn't?"

"You start a new school and you give up the space games, all right?"

"No," Thomas said, "I won't."

"No more eating out of tubes." Mr Moon set down his knife and fork and made his points with his fingers. "You eat properly. You study. You join in at school. You engage with the real world, Thomas."

Mrs Moon cleared away. Thomas engaged with his pudding. Miserably punting his treacle sponge through log jams of custard, he thought about things he could say. He could point out his father's own peculiar habits, but how helpful would that be? *Mission Control, come in, please. We have an asteroid belt. Lumpy custard ahead, plus major parental-type bumps.*

Then something started to happen outside. In fact, it started inside. Inside the Pughs' back kitchen. Through their own kitchen window overlooking the Pughs' back door, Thomas and his mother and father could hear a commotion heading up inside the Pughs' place like a giant boil about to burst. Someone shouted sharply. *"Leave it – Adrian, get away!"*

Mrs Moon got up. "What on earth's going on over there?"

The sound of furniture rocking and scraping

as someone got out of someone else's way in a hurry was followed by major bumping and banging noises and yet more sudden shouts. The Pughs' back door shook visibly as someone fell against it.

Thomas felt a rush of fear. "Is Adey all right? What is it?"

Suddenly the Pughs' back door burst open. Mrs Pugh rushed out screaming. Adey scuttled after her holding both his arms over his head, making a thin, quavering sound horrible to hear. After them both roared the monster Pugh, mad as a bull, with a belt. A belt he lashed at Adey. Adey clung behind his mother. *"No, no, Dad, doan hit me!"*

Mrs Pugh pleaded and screamed. *"Don't, John, he never meant to!"* She tried to fend him off with her arms. Adey dodged and whimpered. *"Please, Mum, doan let him hit me!"* Monster Pugh lashed and swore. He tore at Adey's legs. He tore and swore and roared. He hardly seemed human at all.

Adey's mother screamed, *"Get behind me, Ade!"* Adey dodged and whimpered. *"Doan let him, no, no, no!"* The bull-monster lunged and roared. Mrs Pugh jumped and screamed. Adey clung and whimpered. Round and round they went, locked in a horrible dance outside their own back door. Inside, their kitchen gaped. Everything stood in mortal dread. The mortal dread had exploded outside. The house was too small to contain it.

"John, don't, please, don't – "

Mrs Moon swallowed. "This is horrible."

"John – you'll kill the boy – no!"

"I can't bear it – I'm going out to stop it."

Colin Moon jumped up. "No, Lyn – don't get involved. These are rotten kind of people."

Thomas Moon looked up. He could hardly hear his parents speak. He looked from one to the other. *We have an outside mission. Requesting EVA.* He felt completely numb. Completely numb for Adey.

"Rotten for Adey," his mother was saying. "I'm not standing by while they beat him."

"They won't thank you for it."

"But Adey will."

"Please, Lyn, don't—"

"Try and stop me."

Mrs Moon set her jaw. She was preparing to EVA into totally unknown territory. The words of the Space School EVA briefing ran madly through Thomas Moon's head. *When astronauts go outside their spacecraft, they wear multi-layered suits to protect them from space hazards, such as micro-meteoroids or anything else that might hit them –*

"Mum! Wait! He might hit you!"

Mrs Moon turned and went out.

"Mum! Be careful, Mum!" Thomas shouted after her.

But his mother had gone EVA already. And

there was nothing he could do to stop her.

Outside the spacecraft window the scene unfolded. Thomas heard the echoes in deep space, where nothing could hurt him. The astronaut approached the site of trauma in slow motion, it seemed to Thomas, leaving no lifeline behind her. *Assistance not required.*

"I've seen the marks on that child!" he heard through the window.

Three figures turned in slow motion. The astronaut raised an accusing arm. "Don't you *touch* that boy with a belt!"

Mrs Pugh fell back. "You keep out of it, missus! It's got nothing to do with you!"

Colin Moon held his head. "Be careful, Lyn," he groaned.

The astronaut drew herself up. "If you ever touch that boy again, I'll report you to Social Services!"

"SHUT THE HELL UP!" the monster bellowed.

"You keep out of it, missus."

"WHAT THE HELL'S IT GOT TO DO WITH YOU – "

"I'm warning you – "

"Oh, shut up."

" – if I see *another mark* on that child – "

"YOU WANT TO MIND YOUR OWN BUSINESS –"

" – I'm going to call the police! Don't you *dare* touch that boy again!"

"Get inside, Adrian," Mrs Monster said. Then she turned on the Monster. "Leave it, John, go in."

The Monster grunted and turned. Trailing its belt, it went in. It had clearly been drinking a bit. It would have liked to have got the astronaut on her own and shown her a thing or two. Dimly, it knew it was in the wrong. As things were, it was shamed...

Adey ducked inside. His mother ducked in after him. Then she slammed the door. No one had met anyone else's eyes. No one had made a lot of sense. But everyone knew what had happened.

Colin Moon opened the window. "That's enough, Lyn, come in!"

The astronaut turned triumphantly. Back in the spacecraft, Thomas Moon watched her return. Something happened inside his heart. With a rush, he knew what it was. *His mother had rescued poor Adey.* Nothing would ever be the same. She'd gone out to challenge Black Pugh, when Black Pugh might easily have hit her. It had been a brave thing to do, as brave as any spacewalk. Something that mattered. Something heroic. Something heroic for Adey ...

Mrs Moon came quietly in.

... something that broke through everything else. *His* mother. She'd done it.

"Mum!" he said, "that was *amazing*!"

Lyn Moon sat quietly down. "It was, wasn't it?" She laughed shakily. "Can I have a cup of tea?"

Colin Moon put the kettle on. "It won't make a bit of difference."

"It *will*," Thomas said, fiercely.

"It doesn't matter what you say to a man like that."

"But now he knows that we *know*. Did you see his face?"

Mrs Moon took Thomas's hand in hers.

"Thomas," she said, "have we hurt you?"

"How do you mean?"

"Give me a hug," said Mrs Moon, suddenly swimming in tears. "You go where you like, to school. I don't care where you go."

"I'll work hard," said Thomas, "I'll study – I mean it, I'll study, I will. And I won't do space stuff so much, if I go back to Boundary Road."

Suddenly he realized that he meant it. Why *would* he do space stuff so much when the real world meant real scenes like these?

RE-ENTRY

You have completed the mission and it is time to return home... As the spacecraft slows down, it comes closer to earth and back into earth's atmosphere. The atmosphere becomes thicker and slows it even more. You are still going quite fast though, and friction makes life pretty hot...
— Helen Sharman, *The Space Place*

Nothing was the same after that. Adey ignored Thomas Moon. He'd been told to – or else, of course. But he never even tried to see him, Thomas noticed. Not even the times he could have.

Wayfinder Three had shut down for good. No bullet head appeared at Thomas's window. No one trailed after him up the road, or showed him the mysteries of the launderette or the Pools any more, or whistled up the milkman or the postman, the way Wayfinder Three used to do.

Some unwritten rule had been broken. But Adey stood taller, for all that. His father even looked cowed. Sometimes Thomas thought he saw Adey through his bathroom window, or glimpsed him climbing the wall and dropping into his garden, but Adey never called for him again. All Thomas heard from Adrian Pugh were broken notes and scales and fragments of a tune called "Kalinka" through Adrian Pugh's living-room window.

Things moved on pretty swiftly. Soon came the day – the night – before school. A new term awaited Thomas Moon. He pictured French with Mrs Carrier. Then he pictured it without her. It was no use going over it. Mrs Carrier had resigned. How could he possibly work hard in French, where everything said Louise?

He hadn't heard from her in ages. On an impulse, he booted up.

Bing!

YOU HAVE NEW MAIL! the screen announced. One of one messages down-loaded.

OK, Thomas clicked, morosely. Let's see what you've got.

Nothing from

Louise.Carrier@ogre.co.uk.

Only a lonely SPM29 sitting in the INbox like a space turkey.

Oh, well. Might as well open it.

Return-Path: <SPM29@starlight.ac.uk
From: <SPM29@starlight.ac.uk
To: <Thomas.Moon@gremlin.net
Date: Mon 7 Sep 11:03:49 GMTOBST
Subject: Re-entry
Astronaut Moon
Congratulations!
So you made it out of orbit. Re-
entry's the hardest part. Your re-
entry module has already separated
from the rest of the spacecraft.
Remember to point your heat shield
towards the direction of flight.
Your capsule is designed to use
the atmosphere as a brake as it
falls back to earth. As you
approach earth's atmosphere you'll
be feeling heavier and heavier.
Good luck —
Bing! You Have New Mail!
- Good luck
Space Control

What was the incoming *Bing!* Thomas wondered. An SPM29 was cool, but an incoming
Bing! was cooler.

Thomas downloaded mail.

It was only a message from Mint:

```
Return-Path: <Mint@Mint.ogre.co.uk
From: Mint<Mint@Mint.ogre.co.uk
To: Thomas.Moon@gremlin.net
Date: Tue 8 Sep 21:32:09 GMTOBST
Subject: To See U Nice
You Spaceman,
Guess what? We're only coming down
for half-term!!!!! Mum and Dad are
staying with Nan!!!!! So can I
stay with you?????
We could go bombing or anything
you like.
It could be really cool.
Mint
```

It wasn't for very long. But it sounded like he meant it. Like he really wanted to come. Thomas Moon felt heavy and full of blood. This was what landing felt like. Real people pulling you back to them. It felt strange. But good. Really good.

"Thomas?"

"What?"

A mug of hot chocolate appeared round the bedroom door.

"Can I come in?"

"'Course."

Mrs Moon took in Thomas's bedroom. The books and bags sorted for school next day. The football kit on the floor. "Here. Drink it up while it's hot."

Thomas sipped his hot chocolate gratefully. He'd been hungry for days on end. Making up for something. Three or four weeks in space. It wouldn't be over till re-entry next day. He would need all the hot chocolate he could get. Fasten your seat-belts, he thought. How will Quinlan be tomorrow? Would everything from last term be forgotten? What about Mr Sumner? Mr Sumner'd be mad as hell.

At least he wasn't alone. Tedious and Barry and Neil would have to go through it, as well. Except for his spacewalk across the school playing fields, none of them, Thomas Moon included, had been in school since the day of *The Merchant of Venice*. Instead, they'd been in the papers and then in the dog-house – arf! arf!

Their first assembly back was going to be grim. On their first day back in school Thomas Moon and the rest of the dog-house posse would stand out like stupid turnips, or like cabbages in a row. There was no escape from assembly, no matter what note you took in. Mr Quinlan was a stickler for lining up the whole school in symmetrical rows and spitting over those rows he could reach, and boring the rest to death. School assembly was already a torture for Thomas. As each class turned to file out at the end, always his blush was rising. The more he tried not to think about it, the more the panic welled up. By the time 9G turned on its heel to face him, he was almost always beet-root red. Thrills of panic raced down his back. His mouth felt dry, his palms wet. His neck throbbed with the full heat of the blush that almost every day would make him stand out to himself, if not to everyone else. As if being singular and knowing it wasn't bad enough, now he had a real reason to stand out. What would assembly be like for those who had been suspended?

Thomas knew he would probably blush no matter what he did. He dreaded those blushes. They crept up from somewhere under his chin and set his ears aglow. The more he dreaded the glow, the more it seemed to happen. Maybe he could turn up his collar. *Remember to point your heatshield towards the direction of flight.* Could he stand the heat of re-entry?

"Ready for school?" Mrs Moon held Thomas's eyes anxiously.

Thomas Moon smiled. Braver than space-men, he knew, were people who faced their mistakes.

"Ready."

"Proud of you, Mister Spaceman."

"Right back at you, Mum."

"For the benefit of those of you who may have been away over the holidays and whose parents, for one reason or another, may not have received my letter, let me read it to you now."

Mr Quinlan cleared his throat. Who *was* that boy in the front row with the bright red face? Positively incandescent. Wasn't it Thomas Moon?

Dear Parent,

As you may very possibly know, I have not been well for some time. With this in mind, I am taking early retirement, as I am unable to give the school the first attention it deserves. I have enjoyed my tenure as head teacher immensely. May I extend to Boundary Road Community School my very best wishes for the future.

Mr Quinlan folded away his letter and scanned the hall. His eyes fell on Thomas Moon. Thomas Moon's ears burned. He could hardly believe what he was hearing. Weird assembly, or what? Was Quinlan *actually saying goodbye*?!

"When a car needs tuning, it's back to the motor mechanic. I intend to tune myself. Then the business of life can go on. You may be going along the Road of Life when suddenly you meet a fork – which path will you take? Should you look back, or pause? Will you reach the castle? Is there a car coming up behind you? Can you –" Quinlan paused "– can you climb the hill?"

"First I've heard of him not being well," Neil hissed to Barry.

"I need hardly tell you all how much I shall miss Boundary Road. But the school must come first. There can be no weak links in the chain. One weak link taints the barrel. One apple, I mean. And so."

"So what," hissed Barry to Neil.

"And so it's my painful duty to have to tell you now that this will be my last assembly." Mr Quinlan adjusted his glasses. "Mrs Carrier will be acting head teacher until Christmas –"

Mrs Carrier! Thomas did a double-take. There she was! In one of the staff chairs onstage!

" – when a permanent appointment will be made. It isn't the way I would have liked to say goodbye to you all. But life, I always say, is like a merry-go-round –"

"He *doesn't* always say that," Neil hissed to Barry. "It's like a bicycle, usually."

"It takes you around and it brings you back. It's up to you to hold on. To understand where you've *been*." Mr Quinlan scanned the hall meaningfully. "I hope you'll hold that thought. Thank you. And goodbye."

He gathered up his papers sharply. He might have announced a change in cake fillings in the High Street for all the emotion he displayed. He really was eccentric, Thomas thought. Unemployed now, too. He couldn't feel sorry for Quinlan. Quinlan could stand in a corner and carry on about the Road of Life and bicycles all he wanted, now that no one actually had to listen. He couldn't bore anyone to death any more. That was all that mattered.

But something else mattered, as well.

Mr Quinlan stood down with his papers. Mrs Carrier got up to replace him. Thomas felt like cheering. *Quinlan out! Carrier in!* His heart might have swelled with pride.

"Thank you, Mr Quinlan." Mrs Carrier smiled. Her eyes fell on Thomas Moon. "I'm sure we'd all like to wish Mr Quinlan a happy retirement."

"I'm sure we *wouldn't*," hissed Neil.

"I'd like to use this time productively. As part of a new strand in school assemblies, people talk about their lives. Today I've been lucky enough to persuade Mrs Innes to be our first Real Lives guest. I think you'll enjoy what she has to say. Mrs Innes. Please."

Trust Mrs Carrier to kick off with a brilliant idea. Real Lives was cool, Thomas thought. *Real* people, telling you what they did. Not teachers waffling on. Mrs Innes – *his* Mrs Innes – began to speak. She had a good speaking voice. Fine. Strong. Dark brown, like Indian tea, full of fascinating Indian words and hints of a jewelled past. Thomas listened spellbound. Born in In-juh, she'd been a soldier's daughter. Her parents had left India and come to England when she was still only small. She'd always wanted to be an actress, but because she was partially sighted, everyone had said she couldn't do it. But she hadn't let that stop her. She'd ended up directing plays. She'd even directed Shakespeare. She enjoyed Shakespeare's plays to this day. Except for *The Merchant of Venice*. She never *could* warm to that play.

Thomas Moon beamed back at Mrs Innes, and didn't care what anyone thought. He'd have acted it out for her if she'd asked him, he was that pleased she'd really forgiven him.

After assembly the bell rang. Thomas Moon met Mrs Carrier in the corridor.

"Mrs Carrier –"

"Thomas."

"How did you – I mean –"

Mrs Carrier smiled. She linked arms with Mrs Innes.

"Did you like Mrs Innes's talk?"

Thomas grinned. "Hi, Mrs Innes. It's just, I wondered how –"

"How?"

"How did you fix Mr Quinlan?"

"Mr Quinlan took early retirement."

"But how did you get your job back? I thought you resigned last term."

Just then, Quinlan walked by.

"Walk *on the left* if you please," he barked, scattering a group of Year Nines out of habit. He nodded briefly as he passed. "Mrs Carrier.

Thomas." He walked on, his kipper tie flapping.

"There's something strange about that man," Mrs Innes said.

"His glasses." Mrs Carrier looked at Thomas. "One of the lenses of his *glasses* is missing."

"You're right," Thomas said, "it was."

No wonder he looked bizarre. One of the lenses of Quinlan's stupid little half-glasses had fallen out and he'd come into school without noticing. It was probably the tip of an iceberg so huge you couldn't imagine. Quinlan was probably one of those people who had milk bottles crowding his step or half a motorbike in his bedroom or a row of woolly hats on his clothes-line and never anything else. Looking through half his glasses and not even noticing the difference – bonkers or what? He'd been half round the bend for as long as Thomas could remember. Now he'd gone all the way round. The bend was a distant memory. Quinlan was coming round again.

Mrs Carrier shook her head. "You can't feel sorry for him, can you?"

"No," Thomas said, who never had any intention of trying, "you can't."

"Especially since he held back my letter," Mrs Innes put in. "It really was quite unprofessional. That's what the Governors said."

"That's how I got my job back, you see." Mrs Carrier cleared her throat. "Mrs Innes

217

gave me a copy of the letter she wrote to Mr Quinlan."

"The letter he never mentioned."

"The letter Mrs Innes wrote, saying you'd called to say sorry, and could he drop your suspension? I took it to Mr Pringle. Mr Pringle was quite annoyed. All that fuss with the papers, he said. Quinlan's made a fool of us. It might have all been avoided."

"So then Mr Pringle sacked Mr Quinlan?"

"Mr Pringle couldn't. But *all* the Governors together could strongly advise he step down. And that's what I think they did."

"They did?"

"They rang me and asked me back three weeks ago. But I thought I'd surprise you today."

"You did surprise me," Thomas said. "You really surprised me a *lot*. It's great you're back, Mrs Carrier." His face fell. "I just thought of something."

"What?"

"I'll have to work in French now. I'll have to try really hard."

Mrs Carrier's eyes sparkled. "Life, you know, Thomas, is like a space flight."

Thomas laughed delightedly. Didn't he know it. It *was*.

"You go up in space – high as you like – then you come back to earth."

All the rest of that day in school seemed

poignant to Thomas Moon. The view out of the window over the hockey field, where he'd bounced as Mister Spaceman; Tedious's stupid notes; the back of Barry's head. Even Chemistry seemed meaningful. One day, he'd come back to school and do Real Lives himself. *I wanted to be an astronaut, but because I was thick in school, I didn't think I could... I didn't think I could be anything, but I'm here to tell you –*

What?

What *did* the future hold? For the first time, Thomas could face it. It wasn't so different, Thomas thought, from facing up to yourself. But that wasn't the end of it, oh no. Far from being the end, it was just a beginning. Even Thomas Moon knew it. At the end of any space flight, there had to be debriefing.

DEBRIEFING

The astronauts' mission continues even after the Orbiter has returned. The crew will spend several days in debriefing, recounting their experiences for the benefit of future crews to assist in future training and to add to the space flight knowledge base.

— Http://shuttle.nasa.gov/sts-
75/factshts/asseltrn.html

"Hold it more firmly. That's it."

"Like this?" Thomas Moon held the drawer. "I can do it myself, Dad, I can."

"You probably can – don't mind me helping you, do you?"

"'Course not." Thomas Moon shrugged off the suggestion. *Leave it, can't you, Dad?*

"I thought you could probably do with a hand."

"Thanks," Thomas said, "I probably could."

No, I couldn't, he thought.

The pine chest of drawers for Thomas Moon's newly redecorated bedroom had looked pretty good in the shop. But it came in an unpromising-looking flat-pack of sides and ends and instructions and packets of screws. You had to put it together yourself, and no way would it fit together easily. Especially with two people trying and getting in each other's way.

You had to be a team player, Thomas Moon knew. The days when he stood in a lift alone for three hours at a time were long gone. But no way was Dad a team player. Dad was always the boss, even though he fumbled joints and got things the wrong way round, things Thomas Moon could see right away were going to be the wrong way up. Already he'd shaken the screws out all over the garage floor and Thomas had had to pick them up. He'd pored over the instructions for ages when Thomas Moon could see straight away how to put the drawers together.

At last the first drawer was finished. Thomas screwed on the knobs. It looked pretty good though, he said so himself.

"Pretty good, isn't it?" he said.

"Not bad at all." Colin Moon stood back. "You've got that knob on crooked."

Thomas corrected it. The pine chest of drawers would look pretty good in his bedroom.

A bit of class, instead of the chipboard under-lying the one-time bedroom space station, now ripped out and adding a silver tone to the heaps of old rubbish up at the dump.

The space-station bedroom had been hard to say goodbye to until his father had handed him the lump hammer. Then it had been easy. Thomas Moon had enjoyed lump-hammering the old silver units off his bedroom walls. It hadn't taken long. They'd looked pretty sad when he'd finished. He'd unscrewed the big metal hook in the wall where he'd hung him-self up in his sleeping bag – weird idea, or what? In no time he'd rollered his bedroom walls in Blue Lagoon Silk Touch Emulsion. Then they'd gone shopping for extras. The flat-pack chest of drawers had been Thomas Moon's mother's idea. She hadn't had to put it together, of course. But how hard could that be?

The second drawer was easier. Dexterously, Thomas screwed up the sides while Mr Moon held them together. He had the hang of it now. Mr Moon slotted in the bottom. Thomas screwed on the knobs. He set it on top of the first drawer. Two down, one to go. Then there was the main bit they fitted into – the carcass, his father called it. It sounded more like a dead animal than a thing you slotted drawers into.

"So how did you get the money for the train ticket to Shropshire?"

Thomas sorted screws ferociously.

"The train ticket, Thomas. I'm waiting."

Thomas Moon looked fearlessly at his father, no more, no less, than himself.

"I borrowed Mum's credit card."

"She told me. She got the bill."

"So why did you ask me?"

"To see what you'd say."

"I'll pay her back."

"Two weeks in the shop over Christmas, nine to five, half an hour for lunch, and never do it again."

"Deal."

They winked on for a while, then Thomas Moon took a deep breath. "I think I broke your laptop."

His father frowned. "My laptop isn't broken. I use it all the time."

"Oh." Thomas crouched to assemble the third drawer, his mind working overtime.

"What do you mean, broke my laptop?"

"Sending emails in America. It's expired by now, probably."

"What?"

"Your Crash Defender program."

"That's nothing to worry about." Mr Moon snorted. "Only some piece of protection software. I cancelled it ages ago."

"But it said, 'Your Crash Defender program will expire in nineteen days' – then twelve, then eight, then four – I thought I crashed it or something."

"It doesn't mean a thing. Have you been worried all this time?"

Thomas Moon finished the last drawer triumphantly.

"What," he said, "me worry?"

He stood the third drawer on top of the others. Now it *looked* like a chest of drawers. Last two knobs. Then they were on to the carcass. Mr Moon laid out the parts – back, top, feet. Sides with runners for the drawers to sit on.

Mr Moon consulted his instructions. "So what was it all about?"

"What?"

"That fuss. I think you know."

"Wanting to go back to school?"

"And all the trouble before."

Thomas Moon passed his father the sides of the carcass. He put in a screw before he answered.

"I don't know why I stuffed up for so long. It was like, I *had* to do it. But I didn't want to run away. I wanted to go back and sort it."

"But you made the muddle yourself."

"Like on Mir," Thomas said, "when they pulled out their main computer lead accidentally. Or when they crashed the Progress supply vehicle into the Spektr module."

"Human error, that's what they call it."

"Human error. Right."

Mr Moon looked at his son. "I'm glad you went back to Boundary Road. Box College would have cost us a mint."

"It wasn't the right thing to do, or anything." Thomas Moon grinned at his father. *Mint*. That name again.

"When's Mint coming, anyway?"

"Tomorrow," said Thomas Moon, with all his tomorrows in his eyes.

"Ready?"

Tedious and Barry and Neil and Mint and Moonie braced themselves in a line on top of the wall. At the word they jumped. And the word was

"Bomb!"

The air tore past Thomas Moon as he plummeted off the citadel wall. In a flash the sea parted beneath him. Down he plunged, and down.

He thought he'd never come up. It didn't seem to matter if he didn't. His ears bulged warningly with the pressure, telling him he was *way* underwater. His eyes filled with bubbles, then cleared. Deep under the citadel wall he vaguely registered the kind of rocks that could have – that *had*, only a week or two before – put someone in hospital for ever. Didn't get *me*, he thought vaguely. Didn't … get … me…

Something erupted beneath him and

225

shooshed him up with it to the surface. The sea and the sky broke over his head as Thomas Moon felt he'd explode. He coughed and gasped and spluttered and held onto Mint. Mint helped him find a rock. Thomas Moon sat down.

"Where's Tedious?" he managed.

"Over there." Mint pointed. "That didn't feel so good."

"It *was* good, though," Thomas said. *I won!* beat the pulse in his chest. *I won! I won! I won!*

"You're thinking about the Space School."

Thomas grinned. No one but Mint could have known what he was thinking about.

"I can't believe I won."

"When did you get the email?"

"Last night before you came. First I thought you sent it. Then I realized you didn't."

"Why would *I* send it?"

"Joke."

"Emails are weird," Mint said.

The message was burned on Thomas Moon's brain:

```
Return-Path: <EuroSpace@SpaceEd.ac.Fran
From: Euro Space School<EuroSpace@
SpaceEd.ac.Fran
To: Thomas.Moon@gremlin.net
Date: Fri 22 Oct 17:06:37 GMTOBST
Subject: Lucky Winner
```

```
Congratulations, Space Commando!
WRITE INTO SPACE
You're one of four lucky winners!
Your winning report entitled
"Flight-deck 747" has earned you a
place on the Shuttle Team for the
week starting January 9th, all
expenses paid! Please report Euro
Space School, Monday 9th January,
at oh-nine-hundred hours!
Please confirm you can attend.
David DeMoulin
Director
```

"I never knew you could write stuff," Mint said.

"Neither did I," Thomas lied. Something in his chest *did* know. It had always known he could.

"So will you go?" Mint asked.

"I might. It's cool that I won. I don't *need* to go any more."

"What – are you kidding?"

"It's space games." Thomas shrugged. "I'm not into space games now."

A huge silence grew around them.

"I know what you mean," Mint said.

"You do?"

Mint nodded slowly.

"I used to be into blading, remember? Now I'm not into blading any more."

Thomas Moon looked into Mint's eyes and saw the half-term reflected in them, a glorious half-term, a half-term shared with someone so close you could trust your lifeline to them.

He got up stiffly. Still the pulse beat. *I won!*

"Hey, Neil!" he yelled. "We're going now! *Barry! Coming up Kingburger?*"

SPACE STATION
MOON

Half-term was over. The autumn sunshine toasted the topmost ridge of the playing fields, and away down over the football pitches the entire school population, Years Seven to Ten, dwindled into the distance like a painting. Beyond them Main Block winked in the sun. Soon he'd be back inside it. Thomas Moon consulted his timetable. Double Geography, Maths. But not until after lunch. Right now he could forget all about it.

Thomas Moon basked luxuriously in the late summer sunshine on the field – Indian summer, Mrs Innes would have called it – and tried not to think at *all*. But Mrs Innes crept into his thoughts. He'd been to see Mrs Innes only that weekend. She'd been OK. Quite good, really. He'd pulled up all her runner beans. They'd needed pulling up, now that the season was over. Plus, he'd written some letters. She could write them herself, of course, but dictating was so much easier. She didn't, Mrs Innes had said, know how she'd got on without him.

He rolled onto his elbows and lazily considered the field. The windows of Main Block flashed in the sun. Somewhere over the field or inside the dwindling crowd, Tedious and Neil would have Coke and Monster Munch and Astros, plus they'd angle in first after the bell and bag back seats in Geography, one of them for him. Thomas didn't actually dream in the back seats too much, these days. Mostly he had his head down, busy – as Mr Frickers *would* say – busy doing himself justice, instead. It was a good feeling. The best. Main Block flashed, the figures dwindled, the faint cry of seagulls over the harbour mingled with the burble from school. Everything came together in the eye of the autumn sun that warmed Thomas Moon's back like a pat from some huge parent. Despite its glamour, he'd rejected Box College, and was he ever glad that he had. Smelly old Boundary Road. Smelly old familiar surroundings.

Mrs Carrier! Hey! Thomas waved.

Mrs Carrier waved back. She liked to stroll on the field after lunch, usually with Peter Armstrong or Amy Ratner from the music department. She didn't see why students shouldn't stroll there, too.

Thomas waved again. *Way to go, Mrs Carrier!*

One of the first things Louise Carrier had done as acting head teacher was to throw open the playing fields at lunchtime and make Mr Sumner hate her. Out of bounds during Quinlan's time, the fields were hallowed ground – until Mrs Carrier had said that they weren't. Mr Sumner had sulked ever since, but he had to wear it. Lunchtimes, he spiked his way grumpily over the pitches with a rubbish spike he'd have liked to collect Year Sevens on, instead of Year Seven's rubbish.

Thomas Moon put his chin in his hands. He enjoyed escaping to the furthest corner of the field, just to be alone for fifteen minutes. He had a feeling, these days. All was right with his world and would be, so long as –

What *was* that in the ground right in front of his nose? Thomas Moon scraped it with his nail. It popped out of the earth into his hands – a dirty, but silver-looking, coin. It had to be a joke coin, from a cracker or a joke shop or something. The profile on it looked fake as anything, kind of obvious and lumpy. But still, it said CAESAR AVGVSTVS. A figure danced on the other side, with Roman numerals round it. Thomas jabbed the coin into the ground a few times. That cleaned it off, all right. Then he rubbed and rubbed it with the sleeve of his jumper. It still said CAESAR AVGVSTVS. It still had Roman numerals. It still looked kind of fake. But suddenly he remembered – Boundary Road had been *called* Boundary Road because it sat on an ancient boundary, even a *Roman* boundary. Thomas Moon turned the coin in his hands. Oh, wow.

He held it up in front of his eye. It looked as big as Main Block. Behind it winked Quinlan's office – *Mrs Carrier's* office.

Mr Sumner approached incredibly slowly with his roller which rolled white lines. He wore a white coat and white shoes. His paint-pot slopped in front of him and piddled paint onto his rollers. Behind him a steady white line unfurled. Everything about Edward Sumner said that nothing was going to interrupt it. Especially not Thomas Moon, who lay in his way.

"Didden you hear the bell?" he honked. "I got a pitch to mark out."

Thomas Moon had visions of staying where he was and making Mr Sumner roll an eccentric white line around him, so that astronauts viewing the earth could make out the Great Wall of China and the shape of Thomas Moon, but instead he got up and said:

"Hullo, Mr Sumner."

"Come on now, clear off, will you."

Thomas Moon widened his eyes. "Did you used to go to this school, Mr Sumner?"

"What's it to you if I did?"

"I thought you might have dropped this."

Caesar Augustus winked in the sun. Thomas Moon extended his hand.

"For you, Mr Sumner," he said.

The golden afternoon slipped away, and the walk home from school took Thomas Moon, as usual, past Golding's Hotel. He pictured Richard Tillson inside it, doing his slick PR number in his cheesy-looking suit, and felt something like pity wash through him. You had to reach for the stars to know you'd missed them, he thought.

Down the road, with the sunshine gilding the treetops; in at the gate – the door – *Hi, Mum!* and into his room went the thoroughly grounded Thomas Moon. He lay down on his bunk-bed and let the sound of the piano next door drive everything else from his mind.

dum – dum
dum – dum
dum – *der*
dum – dum
dum – dum
dum – *ber*
dum – dum
dum
dum – dum
bum – *ber*
DUM – DUM –

– wait for it, Thomas thought –

DUM – DUM – DUM
DIDDLE – UM
DUM – DIDDLE – UM
BUM – BUM!

Adey was coming on. His "Blue Danube Waltz" was stirring stuff, Thomas thought, as the sound of Adey's piano practice drifted in through his bedroom window on the lazy, after-school air. He'd been hitting the right notes for quite a while. But now they had *feeling*, as well. It was possible Adey had talent. Thomas had heard his father say so, and *he'd* had it first-hand from Bodger Daniels, Adey's piano teacher, who lived down the road over a junk shop and always wore the same clothes.

dee – dah – dah – dah
dah – dah – dah – dee
dud – de – lud – der – duh
dud – de – lud – *der* – duh –

He's off again, Thomas thought. He pictured Adey rampaging up the keyboard and pounding those RUM-BUM notes. Adey, with the banged-up knees. Adey, who looked taller and colder and older these days, the old Adey somewhere underneath. It was strange to find out that all the time he'd known him, on top of the old Adey there had always been an Adey with talent. An Adey Thomas didn't know.

That was the way the space cookie crumbled, Thomas Moon supposed. Adey had his tune to play. And somewhere, Thomas had his own.

The last few months had been more than strange. The spacewalk on the school field. The mint imperial fight in *The Merchant of Venice*. The trip to see Mint on the train. The flight in the 747, all the way over the Atlantic. Box College – crying in front of the mirror in Speakes Department Store – the dreadful day outside the Pughs' back door, when his mother had done a spacewalk of her own – Quinlan's departure – Monsta Trux – Mrs Carrier's smile.

He was slowing

right

down

in the atmosphere. Catching up with himself. Thomas turned all of it over in his mind and tried to understand what had happened to him, as Adey turned back to "Kalinka". He had "Kalinka" off like clockwork by now. But Thomas preferred "The Blue Danube Waltz".

The Danube so blue –
so blue –
so blue –
Not the blue of space, the blue of a river –
the Danube so blue –
so blue –
except it wasn't blue at all, seeing as how it was so heavily polluted.

Whatever had happened to him lately was pretty indigestible, if he thought about it. Thomas tried to think. There was something he'd forgotten. Something he had to *do*, to knit it all together – what?

He got up and closed the window and put on a tape.

What *about* SPM29? The mystery spaceman? Wasn't it time to say goodbye? Suddenly Thomas Moon knew what he had to do.

Thomas switched on the computer.

FOUND CDROM the screen winked.

Clicking on SHORTCUT TO GREMLIN NET, then CONNECT, Thomas Moon activated dialup networking without even knowing he'd done it.

BEE – WHEEE – DIM-DUM-DI-DUM – the familiar screech of the dialling tone making a connection told Thomas Moon that for once he was in control.

One last time. Let's hear it for Gremlin Net.

Opening Message/New Message, Thomas began to type:

```
Return-Path: <Thomas.Moon@gremlin.net
From: TCM24<Thomas.Moon@gremlin.net
To: SPM29@starlight.ac.uk
Date: Thu 3 Nov 16:10:32 GMTOBST
Subject: Over and Out
MISTER SPACEMAN
Sometimes you have to move on, so
```

this is goodbye. Mission accom-
plished. The end. Cool while it
lasted, huh?
I'm not sure exactly what happened
or how I got into orbit, but I
landed all right and I'm fine.
I've even got some friends left.
Plus I like school a lot more.
Feels like I've been on this long
journey. Feels like a million
miles.
I still want to be an astronaut.
But I'm going to see what happens.
I'm not going to try to force it.
You can only make a Mission State-
ment and hope it works out, right?
There's other things I'd like to
be. I'm going to see how I feel.
Did you know I found an Augustus
Caesar coin in the playing field
at school?
I gave it to Mr Sumner. You should
have seen his face.
Shutting down all connections at
this address.
Over and Out
Thomas Moon

Clicking SEND, Thomas grinned. A message
to himself, *from* himself. How cosmic was
that? The last message to and from Mister

Spaceman. He would find it waiting for him on the library computer at school, under the "starlight" address he'd enjoyed setting up – oh, a long time ago now. Beyond and behind it was the silence of space. A silence he wouldn't break easily. *We copy your departure, SPM29. So long. Over and out.* Thomas Moon deleted previous correspondence in Edit Mail. Then he shut down Pandora. Then he called up the hidden TEXT_TXT file lists and deleted bundled TEXT files 1–8. Then he removed SPM29's address from his mailing list for ever.

That was the end of SPM29. He'd been fun while he lasted. The whole astronaut-mysteriously-emailing-you-thing had had a pretty good run. Fantastical spacemen beaming in messages over the wires – why not? So Gremlin Net hadn't always co-operated. Sending emails *to yourself* was quite a tricky business. It involved creating an "address" at school and bundling "secret" messages for yourself despite the resulting confusion. The Gremlin Net had kicked up quite a bit. It had tried to dob him in to his dad. It didn't like hiding TEXT files. It didn't like being used.

But Thomas Moon had done it. Spun his elaborate web. Bent his life to a dream. He'd always made things up, as far back as he could remember. He'd always dreamed out of windows. Written things down in notebooks.

Lived whatever he read. An overactive imagination, that was what everyone said. What could you do with an overactive imagination? You could make things up, that was what. Making things up left you in control of what happened. You could make up anything you wanted.

Being in control was cool. It left Thomas Moon free to imagine – to *be* – anyone or anything he liked. It was better than steering a starship. Better than being an astronaut. Astronauts had to have lifelines. Thomas Moon was his own lifeline. Instead of an astronaut, he might turn out to be a person who dreamed up SPM29s all the time. He might make up *whole new worlds* for himself and other people, out of the everyday stuff around him that wasn't fantastical at all. That was a job for a *real* space cadet. Inner space. The final frontier. There had to be a story in that.

Opening WORD, DOCUMENT/NEW DOCUMENT, Thomas began to type. Ideas flew down from his brain to the screen, flooding the screen with words. Characters crowded at his elbows, spacemen sucked oxygen behind him, stone-age warriors rattled the door to come in, mournful-looking aliens flashed messages across their heads and pointed out his mistakes.

Thomas Moon's fingers flew. He liked the way he could dream up worlds. One day he might be a writer.

WEATHER EYE
Lesley Howarth

Telly Craven is a Weather Eye, part of a club that shares information by computer about climatic conditions around the world. And, as 1999 ends, weird things are happening: floods, earthquakes, force ten gales... It's during such a storm that Telly has a Near Death Experience, leaving her with strange psychic powers. Now she is *the* Weather Eye with a clear, if daunting purpose...

"Often very funny... It is subtle, sophisticated and beautifully written... It must reinforce Lesley Howarth's position as one of the best novelists now writing for young readers."
Gillian Cross,
The Times Educational Supplement

"Outstanding... A degree of suspense and pace that would do credit to Raymond Chandler."
The Independent

THE PITS
Lesley Howarth

Gang warfare in 7650 BC.

Things weren't so different back in the late Stone Age. The weather may have been colder but, as the ghost of Broddy Brodson will tell you, human behaviour was pretty much the same. And he should *know*. For Broddy was a member of the Axes gang that fought the Pits for control of the sandpits that last, crazy, turbulent summer. He *knew* Ma Fingers, Treak the Bedeviller, Vert and Hayta, 'Viger Wildgoose, Cud, Eels, Argos, Arf... And now he's going to tell you the whole, incredible story!

"This is a sparky, humorous story, with a fast-moving plot... Lesley Howarth thinks big, and this is a big, challenging book." *Gillian Cross, The Times Educational Supplement*

MAPHEAD
Lesley Howarth

Greetings from the Subtle World –

Twelve-year-old MapHead is a visitor from the Subtle World that exists side by side with our own. Basing himself in a tomato house, the young traveller has come to meet his mortal mother for the first time. But, for all his dazzling alien powers, can MapHead master the language of the human heart?

Highly Commended for the Carnegie Medal and the WH Smith Mind Boggling Books Award.

"Weird, moving and funny by turns... Lesley Howarth has a touch of genius." *Chris Powling, Books for Keeps*

"Offbeat and original... Strongly recommended to all who enjoy a good story." *Books For Your Children*

THE FLOWER KING
Lesley Howarth

The narrator of this story doesn't just see colours, he *feels* them. At home, the colour is mainly panic-button red. But on Saturdays, visiting old Mrs Pinder, a hopeful yellow floods in. It's the yellow of the daffodil fields where "Pinny" worked as a child for William Bowhays Johns, the Flower King, whose tragic story lies at the heart of this absorbing tale.

Shortlisted for the Whitbread Children's Novel Award and the Guardian Children's Fiction Award.

"Characterization is deft, the descriptive passages lyrical, the dialogue tone perfect."
Michael Morpurgo, The Guardian

THE MIDWINTER WATCH
John Gordon

One winter's day, a hundred years ago, a valuable timepiece was stolen from Silas Heron.

The theft was blamed on a passing beggar boy – but, as Sophie, Jack and Simon are about to discover, the truth is far more complex. With the arrival of a sinister stranger at the village's abandoned railway station, secrets from the past and present combine to test the children's ingenuity and courage to the full.

"The perfect book for curling up with in front of the fire... It has a timeless and classic feel... A brilliantly inventive story." *The Guardian*

"Engaging supernatural thriller... An enjoyable tale with all the traditional Christmas trimmings." *The Independent on Sunday*

THE BEAST OF WHIXALL MOSS
Pauline Fisk

At the age of eleven, Jack is resigned to his world.

So what if he can never satisfy his mother's desire for perfection and his brother can? So what if he's lonely out on Whixall Moss? He doesn't care – or so he likes to tell himself. Then one day he sees, in a boat hidden on the creek, a beautiful, fabulous beast. At once he is filled with a wild longing: he must own it. But the boat's mysterious inhabitants have other ideas…

Gripping and powerful, this novel by Smarties Book Prize Winner Pauline Fisk is a tale that will live long in the imagination.

FIRE, BED AND BONE
Henrietta Branford

The year is 1381 and unrest is spreading like plague.

England's peasants are tired of the hardship and injustice they suffer at the hands of harsh landlords. Rebellion is in the air, bringing dramatic and violent upheaval to the lives of families like Rufus, Comfort and their children – and even to dogs, like the old hunting bitch, who is the narrator of this unforgettable tale.

Winner of the Guardian Children's Fiction Prize and the Smarties Book Bronze Award, this extraordinary story depicts the tumult and tragedy of the Peasants' Revolt through the eyes, ears and nose of a dog.

GIANTS
Hugh Scott

A giant head staring from a toyshop window. A bookseller who eats his books. Teachers whose limbs stretch to impossible lengths. What can it all mean? Harry's dad once said that the town's huge cathedral was built by giants, but he didn't really mean it, did he? There are no such things as giants ... are there?

This is an entertaining and suspenseful story by the author of the award-winning *Why Weeps the Brogan?*

MY LIFE AS A MOVIE HERO
Eric Johns

In times of crisis, Owen Royston Barron is a hero.

Well, in the interactive movies that run in his head he is. In real life he feels more like a worm. "Look after Mum," his dad said – and what did Owen do? He encouraged Mum to move in with slobby, loud-mouthed Frank. Now Owen is out on the street with his mum and wonders if he'll ever be able to get things straight. Will he always be two people – one inside, one outside? Can he ever redeem himself for what he's done? As absorbing and entertaining as the best screenplay, this is the story of Owen's struggle to bring the movie that is his life to a happy ending.

JOHNNY CASANOVA
Jamie Rix

Johnny Worms is hot to trot, the unstoppable sex machine, Johnny Casanova... Well, so he believes. So when love's thunderbolt strikes in the form of Alison Mallinson or a beautiful vision in purple what can Johnny do? And is it his fault that Cyborg Girl, Deborah Smeeton, finds him irresistible?

"A genuinely funny book, sparklingly well-written." *The Independent*

"The first chapter had me laughing aloud at least three times." *The Scotsman*

SO MUCH TO TELL YOU
John Marsden

Scarred, literally, by her past, Marina has withdrawn into silence.

She speaks to no one. But, set the task of writing a diary by her English teacher, she finds a way of expressing her thoughts and feelings and of exploring the traumatic events that have caused her distress. There is so much she has to say...

"Beautifully written... The heroine's perceptiveness, sense of humour and fairmindedness temper the tragedy and offer a splendid read."
The Times Educational Supplement

"A moving chronicle of personal recovery."
The Observer

THEY MELTED HIS BRAIN!
Simon Cheshire

Schoolboy film-director Matthew Bland makes sensational movies.

With titles such as *Head Transplant*, they all star his friends Lloyd and Julie ... and they're all rubbish. But one morning, at a quarter past three, Matthew's video records a sinister brain-washing TV transmission that's beyond even *his* wildest imaginings! Can Matthew Bland, investigative film-maker, expose the evil doers before the final credits roll?

Fab, funny, fast and furious – these are just a few words that begin with the letter F. Do they describe this book? You'll have to read it and make up your own mind!

DOUBLE VISION
Diana Hendry

"People would do a lot better if they could see double like me... I mean seeing things two ways – with the head and the heart."

Growing up in a small, North West coastal town in the 1950s, fifteen-year-old Eliza Bishop finds life unbearably claustrophobic. But to her small, fearful sister Lily, the seaside setting affords unlimited scope for her imgination. Through these two very different pairs of eyes a memorable range of characters, events and emotions is brought clearly into vision.

"Succeeds totally where very few books do, as a novel which bestrides the two worlds of adult and children's fiction with total success in both... The stuff of which the very best fiction is wrought."
The Sunday Times

TWICE TIMES DANGER
Enid Richemont

Have you seen this girl? Missing from home. Daisie Trevelyan. Aged eleven.

Becca and Daisie have been best friends for two years but their friendship has grown increasingly strained during the summer holidays, before starting at different schools. Then Perdita turns up: posh, bossy, rich Dita, so identical to Daisie they could be twins. And from the moment the two girls meet, Becca is an outsider, a stooge in their games of swapping identities. But what begins as a joke to fool Dita's au pair becomes deadly serious when Daisie goes missing. Who has taken her and why? Becca must solve this sinister mystery to prevent twice times danger turning into double death.

RIDING THE WAVES
Theresa Tomlinson

"Don't let the waves frighten you. They can knock you down, but they can't stop you getting up and trying again."

When Matt goes to visit Florrie as part of a school history project, he doesn't expect to enjoy himself. Why should some cranky old lady's reminiscences interest him? He'd much rather be down on the beach with the surfers, riding the waves – if only he had a board... There's a lot more to Florrie, though, than meets the eye, and her personal history has some uncanny similarities to Matt's own!

"Sparkling, moving and funny." *The Guardian*

MORE WALKER PAPERBACKS
For You to Enjoy